THE COLTONS: COMANCHE BLOOD

Discover a proud, passionate clan of men and women who will risk everything for love, family and honor.

Sky Colton:
Hurt by love before, she only agreed to play Dr. Dominic Rodriguez's fiancée out of overwhelming guilt. Can she survive this time with her heart still intact?

Dr. Dominic Rodriguez:
The no-smiles surgeon doesn't get close to people—he can't afford to as a doctor. But Sky Colton makes him laugh—and feel things he never wanted to....

Gloria WhiteBear:
The truth is out that she was the real wife of Teddy Colton—making the Oklahoma Coltons his true heirs. But this scandalous secret could prove deadly!

Grey Colton:
His great-grandfather calls him the lone wolf—but he feels he has more important things to do than chase after women....

Dear Reader,

Grab a front-row seat on the roller-coaster ride of falling in love. This month, Silhouette Romance offers heart-spinning thrills, including the latest must-read from THE COLTONS saga, a new enchanting SOULMATES title and even a sexy Santa!

Become a fan—if you aren't hooked already!—of THE COLTONS with the newest addition to the legendary family saga, Teresa Southwick's *Sky Full of Promise* (#1624), about a stone-hearted doctor in search of a temporary fiancée. And single men don't stay so for long in Jodi O'Donnell's BRIDGEWATER BACHELORS series. The next rugged Texan loses his solo status in *His Best Friend's Bride* (#1625).

Love is magical, and it's especially true in our wonderful SOULMATES series, which brings couples together in extraordinary ways. In DeAnna Talcott's *Her Last Chance* (#1628), virgin heiress Mallory Chevalle travels thousands of miles in search of a mythical horse—and finds her destiny in the arms of a stubborn, but irresistible rancher. And a case of amnesia reunites past lovers—but the heroine's painful secret could destroy her second chance at happiness, in Valerie Parv's *The Baron & the Bodyguard*, the latest exciting installment in THE CARRAMER LEGACY.

To get into the holiday spirit, enjoy Janet Tronstad's *Stranded with Santa* (#1626), a fun-loving romp about a rodeo megastar who gets stormbound with a beautiful young widow. Then, discover how to melt a Scrooge's heart in Moyra Tarling's *Christmas Due Date* (#1629)

I hope you enjoy these stories, and please keep in touch!

Mary-Theresa Hussey

Mary-Theresa Hussey
Senior Editor

Please address questions and book requests to:
Silhouette Reader Service
U.S.: 3010 Walden Ave., P.O. Box 1325, Buffalo, NY 14269
Canadian: P.O. Box 609, Fort Erie, Ont. L2A 5X3

Sky Full of Promise

TERESA SOUTHWICK

Published by Silhouette Books
America's Publisher of Contemporary Romance

Special thanks and acknowledgment are given to Teresa Southwick for her contribution to THE COLTONS series.

ISBN 0-373-19624-5

SKY FULL OF PROMISE

This edition published by arrangement with Harlequin Books S.A.

Visit Silhouette at www.eHarlequin.com

Printed in U.S.A.

Books by Teresa Southwick

Silhouette Romance

Wedding Rings and Baby Things #1209
The Bachelor's Baby #1233
**A Vow, a Ring, a Baby Swing* #1349
The Way to a Cowboy's Heart #1383
**And Then He Kissed Me* #1405
**With a Little T.L.C.* #1421
The Acquired Bride #1474
**Secret Ingredient: Love* #1495
**The Last Marchetti Bachelor* #1513
***Crazy for Lovin' You* #1529
***This Kiss* #1541
***If You Don't Know By Now* #1560
***What If We Fall in Love?* #1572
Sky Full of Promise #1624

*The Marchetti Family
**Destiny, Texas

Silhouette Books

The Fortunes of Texas
Shotgun Vows

TERESA SOUTHWICK

is a native Californian who has lived there most of her life. Having lived with her husband of twenty-five-plus years and two handsome sons, she has been surrounded by heroes for a long time. Reading has been her passion since she was a girl. She couldn't be more delighted that her dream of writing full-time has come true. Her favorite things include: holding a baby, the fragrance of jasmine, walks on the beach, the patter of rain on the roof and, above all, happy endings.

Teresa has also written historical romance novels under the same name.

THE COLTONS: COMANCHE BLOOD

George WhiteBear

Kay Barkley (d) ? m Theodore Colton (d) m Gloria WhiteBear
See *"The Coltons"*

Sally SharpStone (d) m Trevor Colton (d) —— Thomas Colton m Alice Callahan

Children of Sally SharpStone and Trevor Colton:
- (2) Bram m Jenna Elliot
- Ashe
- (1) Jared m Kerry WindWalker
  - Peggy
- Logan
- (3) Willow m Tyler Chadwick

Children of Thomas Colton and Alice Callahan:
- (7) Grey
- (5) Billy m Eva Ritka
- (4) Jesse m Samantha Cosgrove
- (6) Sky m Dominic Rodriguez, M.D.
- Shane
- Seth

(1) WHITE DOVE'S PROMISE
by Stella Bagwell *SE #1478 On sale 7/02*

(2) THE COYOTE'S CRY
by Jackie Merritt *SE #1484 On sale 8/02*

(3) WILLOW IN BLOOM
by Victoria Pade *SE #1490 On sale 9/02*

(4) THE RAVEN'S ASSIGNMENT
by Kasey Michaels *SR #1613 On sale 9/02*

(5) A COLTON FAMILY CHRISTMAS
by various authors *On sale 10/02*

(6) SKY FULL OF PROMISE
by Teresa Southwick *SR #1624 On sale 11/02*

(7) THE WOLF'S SURRENDER
by Sandra Steffen *SR #1630 On sale 12/02*

LEGEND:
m Married
d Deceased
—— Twins

Chapter One

"You don't look like a home wrecker."

The sound of the deep male voice turned Sky Colton quickly from the sales receipts she'd been totaling. She hadn't heard anyone enter the store. Since Christmas the previous month, her high-end jewelry business in Black Arrow, Oklahoma, had been slow. Facing the tall, dark, handsome stranger, she wondered if sales were about to pick up. Along with her heartbeat.

Then his words registered. She folded her hands and rested them on the locked glass case containing her exclusive, original jewelry designs. "Home wrecker? If you're not looking for a demolition company, I have no idea what you're talking about."

"Right. And mermaids can do the splits."

Sky studied him more closely. His worn black leather bomber jacket was at odds with the powder-blue, button-down collar shirt tucked into his jeans. She couldn't help noticing his abdomen was washboard firm. No beer belly or love handles. His dark brown hair was cut conservatively short. It was the dead of winter, yet his olive skin made him look tanned. And she expected his eyes to be warm brown, like hot chocolate. They weren't.

Instead they were dark blue and sizzling with anger. Why? What had she done to him? She'd never seen this man before. She was sure of it.

"I would remember you," she said, then winced. Nothing like nourishing the ego of the man who was looking at her as if he wanted to stake her out on the nearest anthill. "If we'd ever met," she added.

"We haven't."

"It doesn't take a mental giant to see you're annoyed. Is there anything I can do for you?"

"Haven't you already done enough?"

She straightened to her full five-feet-six-inch height, but that didn't do much for her intimidation quotient. He had the advantage of another six inches and pretty much towered over her. Quite an attractive tower, she couldn't help noticing. And if he weren't so crabby, she might have been tempted to flirt.

"Look, Mr.—" She waited for him to supply a name, but he didn't. She sighed. "The only thing I do is design and sell jewelry. I use Native American elements in my designs, which some people find mystical. But I'm not psychic. You're going to have to give me more information if you expect me to undo any injustice you think I've done you."

"I don't think it. I know it."

"What?"

He reached into the pocket of his jacket and pulled out two black-velvet jewelry boxes, then set them on the glass counter. Curiouser and curiouser, she thought.

Sky picked one up and opened it, noting her business logo embossed on the lid's satin lining. The ring inside was definitely her own design and one of her favorites. It was a gold band that she'd created for Shelby Parker, a wealthy oilman's daughter from Midland, Texas. She'd become engaged during the holidays to a man she'd known a short time and her fiancé had wanted the wedding arranged quickly.

After hearing about Sky's designs from a friend, she'd had her chauffeur drive her from Houston to Black Arrow to personally commission wedding bands. Her fiancé hadn't had time to buy her an engagement ring or to accompany her to shop for this very important purchase. Shelby had returned several times, to make adjustments to the designs and talk about her ideas for bridesmaids and groomsmen gifts. Always, the chauffeur had driven her, making Sky wonder if she were as flaky as a soda cracker or just afraid to fly.

Sky remembered the young woman chattering away while she'd roughed out some ring sketches. Then again when they'd discussed changes to the designs, Shelby had wondered about using gold as opposed to silver or white gold, and possibly adding precious stones. Now Sky struggled to recall snippets of the conversations. Shelby had said her fiancé was a well-known Houston plastic surgeon. His name was—

She could only recall that Shelby had joked about calling him Dr. StoneHeart. Sky couldn't remember his real name and opened the other box, plucking the large men's ring from it. Subtly etched into the gold were the initials D.R. She had the most inane thought about the irony of his initials spelling out his profession. Then, she looked up from the ring in her hand to eyes growing angrier by the second if the darkening blue around his irises was anything to go by.

"Dr. Dominic Rodriguez," she said. She held out her hand. "It's nice to finally meet you. I'm Sky Colton."

"I know," he answered coolly.

"Shelby told me a lot about you." Most of which she couldn't remember.

"Interesting you associate your clients by pieces of jewelry."

Sky didn't much care for his tone. "I've seen enough medical dramas on TV to know that doctors identify their patients by symptoms or diagnosis. Frankly, my way is far more pleasant. Wouldn't you agree?"

One corner of his mouth turned up, but that was her only indication that he was even the tiniest bit amused. "No."

"My sincere and heartfelt congratulations on your upcoming wedding. Obviously you're here because you'd like some changes on the rings. I can—"

"I'm here because there's not going to be a wedding."

Sky blinked up at him. "No wedding? But I don't understand. Have you and Shelby postponed—"

"I believe the words were quite clear. But let me rephrase. The wedding is off. Permanently," he added for emphasis. "I received a bill for wedding bands. And for groomsmen gifts in progress."

Sky stared at him, mortified that she couldn't stop herself from noticing how dangerously sexy he was. She sensed in him a leashed intensity that could change to passion in a heartbeat. If provoked. Or maybe she was overdue for an appointment with a shrink. For goodness' sake, the poor man had just been dumped. Or had he? Maybe *he'd* called it off.

Studying the tension in his jaw and the stiff set of his shoulders, added to the angry gaze and sarcastic tone, she decided she'd been right the first time. Definitely dumped. And he wasn't the least bit happy about it.

For good reason. He'd practically been married. But "almost" wasn't a done deal. Why should that please her even a little bit? Good question, for which she had no answer. Since her own broken engagement, she'd managed to get on with her life by scrapping her girlish fantasies of marriage, husband, children. Now her goal was to build an already fast-growing business. It was counterproductive to be attracted to this man. Technically he might be available, but emotionally he was still attached to someone who was no longer attached to him. While Sky might think the woman shortsighted, or even blind, maybe mentally impaired if not downright stupid, the fact remained, he was hurt and angry.

But what in the world happened? From what little she could recall of her conversations with the bride-to-be, Sky had the impression that Dr. StoneHeart was perfection personified. What had made her change her mind? Why had Shelby blown him off? Then Sky recalled the words that had alerted her to his presence when he'd walked in the shop. *You don't look like a home wrecker.* What had he meant by that?

"Dr. Rodriguez, I have the impression you hold me responsible for something."

"I do." He laughed, a harsh sound and completely without humor. "Guess I won't be saying that anytime soon. At least not in a church in front of a priest and witnesses."

She held up her hands. "Let's back up for a minute. You said the wedding is off. Why? What happened?"

"Don't play dumb, Miss Colton."

"I'm not playing anything, *Dr.* Rodriguez. I have no idea what's going on. Would you care to enlighten me?"

"I'd like nothing better. Because of things you said, Shelby refused to marry me."

"What I said?" Sky pressed a hand to her chest. "Look, Doctor, when she was here, I was working. We engaged in idle chitchat, not a bare-your-soul, heart-to-heart kind of conversation. I can't imagine what I said that made her change her mind."

"Think."

Sky did. "She told me about you. That you're a plastic surgeon. You help people feel better about themselves. That she was honored someone in such a noble profession would be interested in her. She had a lot to live up to. But she left out—" Sky stopped. She couldn't believe what she'd almost blurted out. Shelby had neglected to mention her intended was a bona fide hottie.

"What?" he asked.

"Never mind. It's not important."

"I'll be the judge of that. What were you going to say?"

Wild stallions couldn't make her tell him. But considering the blue blaze in his eyes, she should come up with a substitute statement.

"She also mentioned that she calls you Dr. Stone-Heart. Although based on your behavior since walking into my shop a few minutes ago, I can't imagine why."

One of his dark eyebrows rose, the only clue that her sarcasm had been noted. "I'm here to settle the bill for your services—including unsolicited advice you gave my ex-fiancée. What else did she tell you?"

"She talked about someone named Reilly Donovan."

"Did she?" he asked, a gleam in his eyes that said he knew the name.

"Yes, I believe he's the chauffeur," she said, her eyes

widening as her voice dropped dramatically on the last word. Uh-oh.

Things were coming back to her. She remembered a little more now. Shelby had also done some talking about the man who'd driven her here. About her intense, overpowering and completely unexpected attraction to the driver. There had been at least four long trips to Black Arrow, Oklahoma, from Houston, Texas. That was a lot of hours in the car—a really big, luxurious car. Lots of time to fill, to talk, to get to know each other intimately, to flirt, to generate doubts. But why did Dr. Perfect blame her?

"Now we're getting somewhere," he said. Leaning forward, he rested his elbows on the glass top of the case as his fingers laced together. "What about the chauffeur?"

Sky noticed his hands. Why in the world would she laser in on something like that when his voice was sharp enough to slice and dice an ice sculpture? But she couldn't help it. He had nice hands, big with long, slender fingers. And strong-looking. And sensitive. The hands of a healer. And, she had a feeling, hands that would know a woman's body and do all the right things in all the right places to elicit passion. The thought made her shiver.

Her only excuse for this behavior was that it had been a long time since Wes Keiler.

Sky met the doctor's gaze, determined to maintain a cool, calm and collected facade even if it killed her. She'd bet the doctor knew some interesting mouth-to-mouth resuscitation techniques.

"Shelby said the chauffeur was handsome," Sky volunteered.

"Now there's a recommendation for a happy life together."

"Don't knock it. Sometimes appearance is our only means of forming an opinion."

"It seems Shelby formed a really good one of Reilly Donovan. She ran off with him. Because of what you told her to do."

"I already told you I didn't tell her to do anything."

Frantically, Sky thought back to the last time she'd seen the other woman. She remembered a sparkle in Shelby's eyes and a flush in her cheeks. The few times they'd worked together, the young woman had always been impeccably groomed. Every hair in place, makeup perfect down to expertly lined lips with color and gloss. Sky envied that. She kept her black hair shoulder-length, in a cut that fell into place after a quick blow-dry.

Now that she thought about it, during their last appointment, Shelby had been slightly agitated, not to mention rumpled. As if a man had run his hands through her hair and kissed off her lipstick. Uh-oh.

"She wasn't herself the last time I saw her," Sky said carefully. "But I made small talk. About how lucky she was—"

"Apparently, Shelby's luck took her in a different direction. It didn't lead her to me." There was bitterness in a tone already liberally laced with anger.

"Oh. Maybe she just got nervous. If you talk to her and reassure her—"

"She left me a note saying she couldn't marry me, after all, and asked me to take care of canceling all the wedding plans. And this bill for the rings," he finished, holding out a familiar receipt.

Sky took it from him and her gaze dropped to the figure on the bottom line. It was a lot of money, but the bands she'd created were lovely, and gosh darn it, they matched perfectly. The time and materials involved didn't come cheap. Now what? Ordinarily she could take back the merchandise and resell it. This set was magnificent if she did say so herself and the profit from it would help in her goal to start another store—maybe in L.A., New York or Dallas.

Before she could respond, the door opened and a male customer entered. With the arrival of the jilted bridegroom, Sky had forgotten this appointment. She'd agreed to design an anniversary gift for his wife.

"I'll be with you in a moment, Clay," she said. Then she met the doctor's gaze. "Look, I can't discuss this right now. I have a previous engagement."

"That makes two of us," he said wryly. "But there's nothing left to discuss. I just returned the merchandise for refund. Our business is concluded."

"We're not finished. I need to give this matter some thought. Where can I reach you later?"

His eyes narrowed, but he said, "I'll reach you."

The next thing Sky knew he was gone. The tall, dark, handsome man was no longer a stranger. And she was destined to meet him again. She should have misgivings about it, but she didn't. Which just proved that she was destined to be the subject of bad country and western songs: "Wanting Men Who Don't Want Me" or "The Only Ring She'll Get Is a Wring Around Her Neck." Because there'd been nothing the least bit romantic or even positive about her encounter with Dominic Rodriguez, except that one small hint of a smile when she'd challenged him about knowing his patients by their ailments.

But for reasons she didn't understand, she was looking

forward to her next, probably last, and possibly explosive encounter with Dr. Dumped.

Shivering in the January wind, Dom waited on the sidewalk outside Sky's the Limit Designs. It was located on Fourth and Main, just down the street from Black Arrow's fire-damaged courthouse. She'd worked with the male customer who'd interrupted them until well past closing time.

From his car across the street, Dom had been able to clearly see through the windows as Sky had shown the man several pieces from her jewelry cases. Finally she'd pulled out a pad and made some drawings. The guy had left and she'd locked the door behind him, then put sheetlike coverings over the cases and did something with the cash register.

Dom had left his car and waited outside because—

He'd been on the outside looking in all his life? He shook his head at the ridiculous thought. Maybe as a kid, but not since making a name for himself as a doctor, a plastic surgeon who specialized in skin grafts and scar reduction for serious burn cases. Which didn't give him immunity since he'd been burned by Shelby a few days before. Odd, but the thought brought less bitterness than he would have expected. Maybe there was good reason for his StoneHeart nickname. Or maybe meeting Sky Colton had blunted the bitterness.

Was that why he'd waited out in the cold instead of coming back tomorrow? Because he didn't want Sky to get away? That was an equally ridiculous thought. She was a businesswoman. Where would she go? All he wanted was his deposit back and for her to write off the balance of the rings. In a long line of details to be handled following his broken engagement, this was the first. And most likely the easiest.

At least on the eyes. Sky Colton was not what he'd expected. For one thing, she was younger. Anyone dishing out advice to the lovelorn as she had should be at least fifty. And not pretty. A meddling person should definitely not have shiny black hair and gray eyes that turned stormy when she was agitated. Or oddly warm and inviting when she was amused. And finally the irritating buttinski who'd wrecked his wedding plans should not be able to make him smile. He'd caught himself just in time.

He didn't want to smile. His orderly life was in chaos thanks to Miss Sky Colton. Things were a big mess and not just because he needed to cancel caterers, flowers, printed wedding invitations and the party to announce his engagement. There was the part that affected people he cared deeply for. Plans that had been a lifetime in the making. Frankly he wasn't sure what to do about it.

After learning that his fiancée had eloped with her chauffeur, he'd been furious. She'd left him a note, along with unpaid bills and deposit receipts for wedding arrangements. But Shelby was gone. That left only Sky as the target for his frustration. He wasn't proud of himself, of the way he'd behaved toward her earlier.

Part of his skill as a doctor came from reaching out to his patients and being able to connect with them on a human level. To understand what they were going through and ease their pain as he repaired damage to fragile flesh. But after rejection, his rage had simmered for several days without an escape valve. Until today. Sky wasn't a patient and he'd reached out in anger.

Because of his brooding thoughts, it was several moments before he realized the lights in the shop were no longer illuminated. The door opened and Sky came out, closed and then locked the door.

Dom stepped out of the shadows. "It's about time."

"Good heavens!" She whirled around and the streetlight nearby showed her surprise. Pressing a hand to her chest, she took a deep breath then said, "In medical school, didn't anyone ever tell you it's not heart healthy to sneak up on a person that way?"

"Sorry." He hunched his shoulders against the frigid wind racing down the neck of his shirt. "Let's just say my common sense is in the deep freeze along with the rest of me."

"You haven't been standing out here all this time, have you?" she asked, incredulous.

"Not exactly. I was in the car for a while."

"Casing the joint? Keeping me under surveillance? Because you thought I might try to skip town?" There was amusement in her voice.

"Along with medical dramas, I think you've been watching too many cop shows."

"Maybe. This may come as a surprise to you, but skipping town never entered my mind. I've got a lot to lose."

"Is that so?" he asked, wondering if losing a fiancée counted for something in her frame of reference.

"Look, reselling the rings could be problematic."

"Why?"

"What are the odds an engaged couple will come in my store with the initials S.P. and D.R.?"

"I don't know what you're talking about."

She frowned up at him. "Did you even check out those one-of-a-kind rings?"

He shrugged. "Why should I? It's not like they're a

sensitive, calibrated medical instrument, or even a stethoscope.''

''Mister, from my perspective when you've seen one stethoscope you've seen them all.''

''I beg to differ. There are many differences, some subtle, some in-your-face.''

''Not unlike the jewelry I create,'' she shot back. ''However I didn't identify you just by the ring I designed for you. It has your initials etched on the inside. At Shelby's request. I'm not planning to hold my breath for a couple with compatible initials to fall in love with each other *and* the matching bands I designed for you.'' She shrugged. ''I might be able to buff out the letters on the inside, but it's still not an item likely to move quickly. I can't afford to keep them in my inventory for long.''

''I see. So you're going to charge me?'' He rubbed a hand across the back of his neck.

''I should,'' she said, sighing. ''Why should I take any responsibility for what your fiancée did? No one ever listens to me. It never even crossed my mind that she would. I was just talking with her, small talk. Generalities. Nothing deep and soul-wrenching.''

''So you said.'' He looked down at her. ''You don't remember telling Shelby she should be excited about her wedding and new life as the wife of a doctor?''

''Vaguely.''

''Do you recall saying to my fiancée life is too short to waste any more than a minute on something that doesn't feel right?''

''Kind of.''

''Did it come up in your general conversation with my bride-to-be that people should follow their hearts?''

"Well, by all means, take me out back and shoot me for dispensing words of wisdom."

"So you do remember that piece of advice?"

"Sounds like something I might've said. What exactly was in the note Shelby left you?"

"That you told her all of the above and she decided you were right. Therefore she couldn't go through with the wedding because her heart led her to Reilly Donovan and they were eloping."

She looked up at him and in the moonlight her eyes seemed enormous. "I don't know what to say except that I'm very sorry your wedding plans didn't work out."

In her gray wool slacks, black turtleneck sweater and matching long winter coat, she seemed so young. He was thirty-eight. Not old. But her fresh youthfulness made him feel ancient.

"Why do you think no one listens to you?" he asked suddenly.

"Hmm?" She blinked. "Oh. I have five brothers—three older and twins younger. I love them, but they just don't have a lot of interest in the things that appeal to me."

"Jewelry?"

She laughed. "For starters." She tapped her lip with her index finger, drawing his gaze to her generous, sensual mouth. "But I usually get their attention when they need a get-out-of-the-doghouse gift."

"Excuse me?"

"When they've done a bad, bad thing and the current woman in their life is ready to give them the heave-ho. If I had a dollar for every time I've come through for them in a pinch, I would be a wealthy woman. Jewelry has saved many a rocky relationship."

"Except mine." But he hadn't been aware that his relationship was on the rocks. Thanks to Sky Colton. "So what are you going to do about the balance I owe on those rings?"

She sighed. "As much as I could use that money, I can't in good conscience collect it from you. There's that whole thing about not kicking someone when they're down."

"Thanks. I appreciate it." He folded his arms over his chest. "I wish all the other wedding arrangements I've got to abort could be taken care of as easily."

Especially in regard to his family, specifically the female members, who would be profoundly disappointed. What was he going to tell his mother? Not to mention his grandmother who'd come all the way from Spain?

"What else do you have to do?" she asked, pulling her coat more snugly around her as the wind kicked up.

"Look, it's freezing out here. What do you say we go somewhere warm and I buy you dinner?"

She eyed him speculatively. "You're not planning to slip a little poison in my grits, are you?"

"Now why would I do that? And just how do you think I could pull it off?" he asked, humor tugging at him again.

"My cousin Willow's friend, Jenna Elliot, is a nurse. By association with her I've learned that nurses and obviously doctors have access to drugs. Have prescription pad, will prescribe."

In spite of his resolve to resist her humor, his mouth curved up. "Did your nurse friend tell you we doctors take an oath to use our powers only for good?"

She laughed again, a merry, cheerful sound. "It's just, you were so bent out of shape when you came in the shop earlier, I just can't help wondering why you'd want to take me to dinner."

He became less angry and more intrigued the longer they talked. On top of that, an idea began to form. It was unconventional, but he had a very immediate problem on the cusp of becoming a crisis. Desperate situations called for outside-the-box solutions. With her help, he might be able to get from Point A to Point B and spend a minimum of emotional energy.

"Let's call dinner a thank-you for writing off my bill," he finally answered, taking her elbow. "Besides, I'm in desperate need of a woman."

Chapter Two

"Hold it right there, Doc." Sky pulled her arm from his grasp. "I'm not that kind of girl."

"No. Wait. You've got it all wrong."

Starting to shiver, she turned up the collar on her coat. "I hate to tell you this, but after a statement like you just made, there's no right way to take it. You're barking up the wrong tree."

"Look," he said, holding his hands up in surrender. "You're going to catch your death out here and I've taken an oath to save lives. Let's go someplace warm where we can talk. I've got a proposition for you."

"And that's supposed to make me feel better—how, Doctor?" She held up her index fingers and made a cross.

"My name is Dom."

"Okay."

"I swear it's not what you think. If I'm lying—"

"What?" she asked.

He shifted his feet on the sidewalk. "Give me a second. I'm trying to come up with something that will convince you of my sincerity.''

''How about if you're lying I turn my five brothers and four big, burly male cousins loose on you. And before you answer, I should warn you, my family is in law enforcement. My father is retired army and then a security consultant. One of those burly cousins I mentioned is the sheriff of Black Arrow. My brother Jesse is with the National Security Agency and Billy is a major in the army. They both know three hundred ways to kill a man with their bare hands. Then there's my brother Grey—a judge. After the rest of them get finished with you, he could send what's left up the river for a really long time.''

By the time she finished, he was laughing. Sky blinked, then stared. She couldn't believe the difference. He went from angry austere doctor to approachable human male in zero point three seconds. Her heart kicked into a lively cha-cha as she noted what a very attractive smile he had. He'd been a hunk-and-a-half a minute ago. Now he was off the scale.

''You think I'm kidding?'' she asked.

She was stalling, trying to sidestep the emotional danger she'd unwittingly unleashed. If she were smart, she would turn on her heel and leave him in the dust. She didn't want to be attracted to a man. Especially one who was on the rebound—a fact for which he blamed her. But she wasn't smart. She stood there and continued to bask in the warmth of his smile until it faded.

''I don't think you're joking.'' He shook his head, but humor still lurked in his eyes and turned up the corners of his mouth. ''I believe you have contacts in law enforcement.''

"So you want to make me a proposition and you don't need a woman, right?"

"Wrong. I want—actually, I *need* to talk to you. If you're offended by what I have to say, bring on the family testosterone."

"All right then. But you don't have to buy me dinner."

Sky trusted this man. Maybe because Shelby had talked about him as if he had wings, a halo and walked on water. Could it be that medical school training in bedside manner helped generate trust in patients? Whatever it was, except for one notable exception when her heart had been the only casualty, she was a good judge of people. Sky knew there was nothing to fear from Dominic Rodriguez.

She angled her head toward the second story above her shop. "My apartment is over the store. I'll cook dinner for you."

"You don't have to do that—"

"You don't think I can cook?"

"No, I—"

She sighed—loudly. "You're just digging yourself in deeper, Doctor."

"I meant no offense." He blew out a long breath, creating a smoky cloud of white between them. "I'm sure you're a fine cook. It's just I don't want to put you to any trouble."

"No trouble. I like to cook. It's relaxing. Besides, it's Friday night. Restaurants in town will be crowded and we'll have to wait. We can be warm and cozy in no time and I'll whip up something that will fill that empty place in your tummy before you can say code blue."

"Code blue?" he questioned, lifting one eyebrow.

"I watch TV."

"So you said."

"This way, Doctor," she said, walking down the alley between her store and the one next door.

"Can't you get upstairs through the shop?" he asked.

She glanced over her shoulder. "No. My cousin Bram—"

"The sheriff?"

"Yes. Bram and my dad checked out everything for security purposes. Since my business is expensive jewelry and a possible target for robbery, they both agreed my apartment should be inaccessible from the store. Just in case."

"Good point. But you still have safety precautions?"

She nodded. "A security system approved by Bram and Dad. Also lots of insurance."

"Actually, I meant your apartment," he clarified.

"I have a separate system upstairs and lots more insurance. No need to worry your pretty head about me." And he did have such a pretty face. But she didn't for one minute believe he was worried about her.

She turned right at the end of the brightly lit alley and led the way up the wooden staircase on the outside of the three-story, red-brick building. At the top, she took the key ring from the pocket of her coat and unlocked the door. After flipping on the lights, she punched numbers into a keypad on the wall, waited for the all-clear beep, then closed the door.

"Home sweet home," she said, removing her coat and hanging it on the wooden tree in the corner. "Can I take yours?"

He nodded, then shrugged out of his leather jacket and handed it to her. It was warm from his body and smelled pleasantly of cologne mixed with man.

"Thanks." Looking around her living room, he said, "Nice place you've got here."

"I like it."

The apartment was spread out over two floors. Upstairs were three bedrooms and two baths, plenty of space for a home office and a guest room if needed. The main floor, where they now stood, was comprised of a living room, dining area off the kitchen and service porch big enough for her washer, dryer and freezer. Her sofa and matching love seat were upholstered in a floral print of green, coral and beige. A glider covered in a coordinating fabric took up a corner of the room with a brass table lamp beside it for reading.

She led the way to the kitchen through the dining room, which was decorated with an ornate oak table with the ball-and-claw feet and surrounded by four chairs. A matching hutch took up most of the one wall.

In the kitchen doorway, she stopped to flip the switch, illuminating the spotlights in the ceiling. "Can I get you something to drink? Beer? Wine? Coffee? Tea?" Me?

Please God, if there was any justice in the world she hadn't just said that out loud.

"Beer would be great."

"Coming right up."

Whew! What was it about this guy that unnerved her so? Enough to invite him up to her apartment. Her personal code of conduct was three dates, minimum, before a guy got the green light to enter her personal space. She hadn't known Dominic Rodriguez three hours and already she was breaking rules.

The refrigerator was on the far wall with a cooktop beside it. The narrow room had countertops on both sides, with a divided sink and disposal bisecting the one on the left. The window above gave her a view of the city of Black Arrow, now lit up for the night.

The heels of her low black shoes clicked on the tile as she walked to the fridge and opened the door.

She leaned over and grabbed a bottle, then straightened and shut the door. When she glanced at him, satisfaction coursed through her as his gaze quickly lifted from her backside. Then she saw an approving look steal into his eyes.

A shiver of awareness skipped up her spine, along with pleasure that he approved of what he saw. But why? She wasn't interested in him and didn't especially care whether or not he was interested in her. She chalked it up to ego. It wouldn't do hers much good to catch him perusing her alphabetized spices in the rack beside the built-in oven instead. She walked the length of the kitchen to where he stood in the doorway.

"Here you go."

Handing him the longneck, she wondered what it was about a man lazily leaning a shoulder against the wall that she found so darned masculine and appealing. He'd rolled the long sleeves of his shirt to just below his elbows, then folded his arms across his broad chest. He could be posing for an ad in a magazine. But he was no male model. He was a doctor who nipped and tucked and made people look like models.

"Thanks," he said, saluting with the amber bottle. "Are you going to join me?"

"You wouldn't be trying to get me drunk, would you?"

"Perish the thought. That three hundred ways to kill a man is an effective deterrent."

"Smart man. Besides that deterrent, it's hard for a tipsy cook to whip up a decent meal."

Turning away from the sexy sight of him casually filling her doorway, she took a plastic-covered baking dish from the fridge and pressed buttons on the oven to preheat.

"That's what you call 'whipping up a meal'?"

"Sure." She glanced to the side and tossed him a grin. "I just whipped it up this morning. Spinach-and-cheese-filled pasta with tomato sauce and herbs."

"Sounds good."

"It is."

She set the timer, then threw together a salad and garlic bread. The only thing left, and she'd been putting it off because it meant breaching his space in the doorway, was setting the dining room table. Here goes nothing, she thought, gathering plates, utensils and napkins.

Sky couldn't decide whether it was fortunate or not that she had to brush past him to get the job done. The very male scent of his cologne was unmistakable and did funny things to her stomach as she passed. If that wasn't bad enough, she was close enough to feel the warmth of his body, making her wonder how she could have been so cold when he'd stood so very near her outside on the sidewalk just a short time ago.

She finished setting the table. "Okay, now we just have to wait until the food is heated. Want to sit in the living room? It's about time to start digging out of that hole you got yourself in."

"Which one was that?"

"You dig so many you can't remember how you offend people?"

"Ordinarily, no. But since I met you—"

"To refresh your memory it was the comment about desperately needing a woman, compounded by the proposition you want to make me."

"Ah, yes."

Sky let him precede her into the living room. Not because she was a Martha Stewart clone concerned about her hostess reputation. She wanted him to pick a couch first so she could sit on the other one, as far away from him as possible. He chose the eight-foot sofa, so she settled herself at a right angle to him on the love seat.

"Shoot," she said. "Why are you desperate for a woman?"

"Actually it's your fault."

"Don't start in on me again," she warned.

"Wouldn't dream of it. But I find myself without a bride."

"What does that specifically have to do with me? Can't you simply move on? I did—"

"What?"

"Never mind. We're talking about you. In your situation, the best thing is to not look back."

"My situation means dealing with my mother. Let me give you a little background and maybe you'll understand." He rested his elbows on his thighs, holding the bottle in both hands between his knees.

"Okay." She sat back and crossed her legs, trying not to notice the second in his seemingly endless repertoire of masculine poses.

"My parents emigrated from Spain when my mother was pregnant with me. My father was a doctor, studying to take his medical boards so he could start a practice in this country. But he was killed in a car accident."

"Oh, dear. I'm so sorry."

Sky leaned forward and put a hand on his forearm. She knew it wasn't a recent tragedy for him, but still felt compelled to offer sympathy. For her that meant touching him. Words only conveyed so much. A reassuring squeeze did far more.

For just a moment he covered her hand with his own. It was the strangest combination of cold and heat. The feeling sizzled up her arm and she pulled her fingers from beneath his palm.

"Because my father had wanted his child to be a U.S. citizen and grow up here, my mother refused to go back to Spain even though her mother urged her to come home. She had no marketable skills, so she cleaned houses."

"A very courageous, industrious woman."

He nodded then took a swallow of his beer. "She put me through college and medical school, supporting us by working as a housekeeper for very wealthy families. The money was pretty good, but every spare cent went for my education. If anyone knew the value of that, it was my mom."

"You must be grateful."

"Yeah." His intense, blue-eyed gaze met her own. "I owe her everything. She gave up a lot for me. The only thing she ever wanted for herself was to travel and to see the world. But she couldn't afford trips and tuition, too."

"She sounds like a wonderful mother."

"If not for the sacrifices she made, I wouldn't be where I am today."

"I agree. But I don't understand what that has to do with needing a woman."

"Patience. I'm getting there." He let out a long breath. "I worked hard to not let her down. Then I was lucky enough to catch the attention of Houston's best plastic surgeon. He offered me a partnership and the opportunity to take over a thriving, prestigious medical practice at his retirement. My own reputation grew fast and for a while now, money hasn't been a problem."

"Yeah, I've heard there's mega bucks in nips and tucks."

"Who knew you could rhyme and be witty at the same time? There's more to plastic surgery than that, but let's save it for another conversation." He rubbed a hand across the back of his neck. "I tried to get my mother to retire or at least let me send her on a trip. Or both."

"And?"

"She's very independent." He shook his head. "She said she couldn't have any fun until I was married and settled down."

"Subtle," she said wryly.

A corner of his wonderful mouth lifted for a moment. "For a long time now my mother and grandmother have made no secret of the fact that, in their opinion, I should be married."

"Mothers are like that."

"That's what she said. Her exact words were that I couldn't possibly understand. It's a mom thing and unless I had a uterus, I would just have to take her word for it."

Sky laughed. "I think I would like your mother. She and your grandmother must have been pretty excited when you got engaged to Shelby."

He nodded. "A whirlwind engagement. It all happened fast, just before the holidays. I wanted to give them two gifts—the news of my engagement and a cruise to Greece."

"Wow." Sky felt her eyes grow wide. Not bad.

"I wanted a small wedding so we could make the arrangements quickly. Shelby agreed. The plan was to bring my grandmother over from Spain. She would accompany my mother on the trip and when they returned, we'd have the wedding."

"What did they say when you told them it was off?"

"Nothing."

"The woman who wished you a uterus said nothing?"

"I haven't broken the bad news to her yet."

"Dom, you have to break the news to her," she said, astonished. "And your grandmother, before she makes the trip for nothing."

"It won't be for nothing if things work out the way I hope. I want to send my *abuelita*—my grandmother—on the cruise, too. My mom would love it. And my *abuelita* hasn't traveled much, either."

"Now that you won't be settled down and married, will they go?" Sky asked.

"If I can get through the party, they won't find out."

"What party?"

"The one to announce my engagement. My mother wouldn't take no for an answer. She insisted her only son have a formal engagement party before she leaves on her cruise."

"That's dishonest. You have to tell them the truth. Surely if they know how much it means to you for them to have fun—"

"That's just it. Even if I can convince them to go under the circumstances, my mother's first trip will start out on a downer. Because of you," he added pointedly.

"Me?" She heard the timer go off in the kitchen and stood. "Thank your lucky stars you were just saved by the bell."

Instead of looking angry or off balance, he merely appeared confident and self-satisfied. "Wasn't that the signal to start round two?"

Sky marched into her kitchen and grabbed oven mitts

then lifted the steaming baking dish out of the oven to a hot plate. "I'm going to say this for the last time. It's not my fault."

But she couldn't suppress the guilt trickling through her. Along with a question that had no answer. If she'd kept her mouth shut and her opinions and advice to herself, no matter how relevant, would his bride-to-be have run off with the chauffeur?

"So you didn't suggest Shelby follow her heart? Or tell her life is too short to waste a minute with anything or anyone who doesn't feel right?"

"I already confessed. And it's good advice, if I do say so myself." Sky had a bad feeling about the way this conversation was going. A diversion would be good. "Dinner is served. Because I promised. After that I think it's time to say good-night."

"Don't you want to know why I need a woman?"

"No."

"You're not the least bit curious?"

"Not a single inquisitive bone in my body."

"You're not a good liar, Sky."

"There's a news flash. Sit down and eat, Doctor."

"I need a fiancée."

"And that pertains to me, how?"

"Just to get through the engagement party."

"Dom, that's only postponing the inevitable. You know what they say."

"No. What?"

"'Procrastination is a crime.... It only leads to sorrow.... I can stop it anytime.... I think I will tomorrow.' It's better to come clean. A clear conscience cuts down stress levels and will help you live longer."

"Thanks for the diagnosis. Normally I would heartily agree with you. But I know those two stubborn women.

If they're not convinced my wedded bliss is just around the corner, they'll refuse to take the trip. And I know how badly my mother has wanted this. On the other hand, if I throw a party, convince them I've never been happier and can't wait to marry the woman of my dreams, my mother and grandmother can go on the cruise without a care in the world."

"Shelby was the woman of your dreams?" Sky asked, her voice small, her guilt compounding by the second.

"My mother would have thought she was perfect. Her family has money. She went to all the right schools. Traveled," he said pointedly. "She's the kind of woman my mom kept house for and grew to admire. Beautiful, independent, educated. Able to take care of herself. Do her own thing and let her significant other do his. Stay in the background while he works. She would have been the perfect doctor's wife."

The ideal mate for Dr. Perfect until Sky had put in her two cents and kiboshed his dream and carefully laid plans. What she wouldn't give for a do-over where she kept her mouth firmly shut.

"So what do you say?" he asked.

"I say you're crazy."

"This isn't a psych evaluation."

Sky shook her head. "It will never work. There are a hundred things that could go wrong. Maybe more." She rested a hand on her hip. "Aren't there laws against this sort of thing? Fraud? Alienation of affections? It's a really bad idea."

"I'm not asking for your opinion."

"Then what are you asking?"

"Will you be the woman? My woman." He looked heavenward for a moment, and let out a long breath. "What I mean is, will you be my fiancée?"

Maybe she was crazy, too, but for a split second she wished he were asking for real. To marry him. How insane was that? "I won't dignify that with a response."

"I'm not looking for dignity. A simple yes or yes will suffice."

"I can't do this, Dom."

"Do I have to remind you it's your meddling that cost me a fiancée? Think about my mother, a courageous woman who sacrificed everything for me. It's my chance to do something nice for her. With your help. Before I have to lay the bad news on her that I'm not getting married, after all. You owe me, Sky."

"When you said you needed a woman, I thought you were talking about something else."

"Like what?" he asked, his mouth curving up to let her know he knew what she meant.

"Sex. I thought you meant sex—as in 'he needed a drink and he needed a woman.' Not necessarily in that order."

"And you still invited me to dinner," he reminded her, his deep voice brimming with laughter.

She sighed. "Yeah. We should both have a psych evaluation. Maybe we can get a group rate." Shaking her head, she met his gaze and sighed. "Sex would have been so much simpler."

Chapter Three

"Yes, but sex won't solve my problem," he pointed out, blue eyes gleaming.

"Then you're certainly different from the average man."

"Thank you."

Sky couldn't believe she'd brought up sex. Was she hoping to distract him from his crazy scheme? Or trying to veer his focus to something more personal? Not happening. Frankly, she would rather he keep trying to turn her into the great pretender. Since she already felt like the family black sheep who didn't fit in, why not pretend to be someone else?

Besides, the idea of getting naked with sexy Dr. Delicious was better than chocolate without the calories, not to mention the benefits of the cardiovascular exercise. Unfortunately, sex wasn't heart smart in the long run. She had tried to fit in with Wes, but he'd wanted her to be something she wasn't. Fortunately she'd found out just before marrying him. At least Dom was up front about what he wanted. That was refreshing.

"Calling you different isn't necessarily a compliment," she said wryly.

"You're changing the subject. What about this—I'll pay for the rings after all. Will you help me out then?"

"It's not about money. Dom, I feel obligated to point out again that this is wrong. Deceiving your mother. *And* your grandmother. It's like tampering with the laws of nature. It's like unleashing the powers of the universe. Maternal powers. Times two. Messing with the woman who gave you life and the woman who gave *her* life." She shook her head. "That's the double whammy. It's a scary thing to do. I just don't know—"

"You're stalling. *And* being overly dramatic."

"I bet you're one of those doctors who doesn't believe in alternative medicine, aren't you?"

"I'm a doctor whose objective is to help the patient feel better using whatever works. If that method is deception, then I guess it can be filed under 'the wrong thing for the right reason.'"

"The end justifies the means?"

"Why not? I told you, I use my powers only for good." He folded his arms over his chest. "What do you say? Mine is a just cause."

"But when they get back from the trip, you still have to tell them the wedding isn't going to happen. It's what they want most in the world."

"It'll happen," he said. "I just need to find another bride."

"Silly me. What was I thinking?" she said, smacking her forehead. "Of course brides just grow on trees."

"I didn't mean it like that. All I need is time to look for someone."

"Like you've got tons of time."

"What does that mean?"

"Your fiancée told me she didn't have an engagement ring because you couldn't find time to shop. And you couldn't find a few hours to come with her to put in your two cents on wedding rings. What makes you think you're going to have the spare time to find another woman to marry you?"

"Can we focus on one problem at a time, please? Or would you like to continue to borrow trouble?"

"If it will prevent you from putting me on the spot, I can keep it up indefinitely."

One dark eyebrow rose. "Are you going to help me or not? Yes or no."

"I can't just give you an answer off the top of my head. It's not that simple." She sighed. "There's a lot to think about. I just don't know."

"I'm going back to Houston on Sunday. Is tomorrow enough time to make a decision?"

"It will have to be."

Sky had no idea why she hadn't simply told him no. Right then and there. No way, no how. Not in this lifetime. But it was too final. And somehow, the simple, two-letter, one-syllable word to end this crazy scheme once and for all would not come out of her mouth.

Procrastination is a crime; it only leads to sorrow. Tomorrow she had to tell him she couldn't impersonate his fiancée. Then tell him goodbye forever. She didn't know when or how it happened, but she would certainly be sorry about that.

The following afternoon Dom paused in the doorway of the Black Arrow Courthouse and surveyed the ravaged building. Black soot covered the interior walls. Evidence of water damage was testament to the efforts it had taken to put out the fire he'd been told had happened several months before.

A little while ago he'd stopped by Sky's shop to see her, but she hadn't been there. The older woman behind the counter who introduced herself as Sky's mother, Alice, had told him where her daughter could be found. She'd volunteered the information that Sky was taking the opportunity to say goodbye to her brother before he left for Washington.

As he wandered through the courthouse, Dom noticed that the damage seemed to be confined to several rooms containing records. The caustic smell of smoke permeated the building and tickled his throat.

Voices drifted to him. He followed the sound, which led him to a wing off the main building and a courtroom untouched by the fire. The bench, witness chair, defense and prosecution tables and spectator seating had suffered no ill-effects that he could see. As her mother had said, Sky was there with three men.

He stopped in the doorway and watched from behind the spectator chairs. With their backs to him, the group continued their discussion, the sound of their conversation echoing loudly in the empty room. Two of the men were roughly his height, which made them about six feet tall. Both had dark hair like Sky's. He'd bet they were two of the "big burlys" she'd warned him about last night and he wondered which one knew three hundred ways to kill a man.

The third guy had different coloring. As Dom stood there, he heard the man say, "Bram, why don't you take care of arranging for damage estimates on the courthouse, the newspaper office and Black Arrow Feed and

Grain. When you have a bottom line, send it to my father.''

Bram ran a hand through his short black hair. Even from this distance the sheriff's badge on his tan shirt was visible. As were the leathers around his waist that included a big gun. ''Look, Rand, I know you're family. But this isn't your problem. Or your father's. I'm sure Joe Colton has better things to do.''

So he was Rand Colton, Dom thought. He'd heard of the wealthy Coltons of California. Apparently Sky was somehow related.

Rand held up his hand. ''It is our problem. My uncle Graham is responsible. Someone in the family is always cleaning up after him, usually my father. Graham is furious about the fact that his father Teddy was never legally married to his mother. But he only hired Kenny Randolph to find and destroy birth records and any other documents linking the Coltons here in Oklahoma with Teddy Colton. Graham wanted money, not mayhem. Although that's what you get when you hire a convicted felon, he never intended for anyone to get hurt or for property to be damaged. Someone from my branch of the family caused the problem and we intend to make it right. Family sticks together.''

''I second that,'' Sky chimed in.

''My father sent me here to take care of it.'' Rand turned sideways, revealing his grin, then he looked at the other two men. ''No one says no to Joe Colton Senior. I don't want to hear any more about it.''

''Whatever you say,'' Bram said, nodding. ''Frankly we're still in a state of shock about the inheritance. Still trying to figure out what to do with it. No thanks to Kenny.''

Rand nodded. ''Jesse, when you get back to Washington, can you use your spy-guy expertise to get a lead on Kenny?''

Jesse nodded. ''I'll see what I can do.'' He looked at Sky. ''Did you distribute that mug shot of Kenny to the rest of the family? Everyone needs to know what he looks like and keep their eyes open.''

''It's taken care of,'' she assured him. ''But he's long gone by now.''

''Don't be too sure, little sister. None of us can afford to let our guard down. He attacked Willow, so we know he's not above harming a woman.'' He glanced at Bram. ''You did check out the jewelry store and her apartment above for security?''

Bram nodded. ''Along with your father. Uncle Thomas agreed the system is state of the art. He insisted on having it monitored. If it's tripped, help will be there in minutes.''

Jesse looked at her. ''Maybe you and I need to go over some of those self-defense moves I showed you—''

''We've got company,'' Rand said, looking suspiciously at Dom.

''Hi,'' he said. The three men turned as one to watch him move closer. Maybe he could use some self-defense moves. He noticed the color that crept into Sky's cheeks when he met her gaze.

Three speculative gazes slid to her as Sheriff Bram Colton said, ''I don't recall seeing you before.''

''Just got into town yesterday,'' Dom explained. ''I'm a friend of Sky's.''

Dom couldn't help thinking this was like a scene from a B Western, where the handsome stranger walks into the saloon. He wondered if Sky thought he was handsome and was surprised when he realized it mattered to him that she did.

He remembered her remark last night about sex being less complicated. He wasn't so sure, but it would probably be dynamite. Studying her now, he noted that flushed cheeks were the only clue that she was uneasy. Otherwise, she was serene and sophisticated. Dressed in a slim black skirt, high heels and a cream-colored sweater that smoothed over her gently curved hips, she looked refined and feminine. Every inch the up-and-coming businesswoman. It was a bonus that she was sexy as hell.

"Dr. Dominic Rodriguez, this is my brother Jesse, my cousin Bram, and Rand Colton, my newfound cousin."

Dom shook hands with the men, then met Bram's black-eyed gaze. "I couldn't help overhearing, Sheriff. Mug shot? I heard you talking about the thug hired by the other branch of the family. But why is Sky involved in distributing his picture?"

"She volunteered." Grimly, Bram looked at the other two men. "The whole family has a stake in catching the creep. He assaulted my sister Willow and damaged several buildings here in town while he was gathering information about us," he said ruefully. "When Graham finally gave up the scheme, Kenny was hung out to dry and he swore to get even with all the Coltons. He's a slippery little weasel and he's wanted for a lot of bad stuff. Until we put him away for good, we all have to watch our backs."

"I see," Dom said. There was enough testosterone in this room to sink a boatload of bad guys. And it was rubbing off on him.

He studied Sky, her clear eyes, creamy skin, shiny black hair. She stood straight and proud and fearless. For reasons he didn't understand, that made him want to keep her close to him so he could protect her. Whoa.

What was that all about? She didn't need him. The thought bothered him and to save his soul he couldn't figure out why.

Still, she was probably right. This Kenny scumbag was no doubt long gone. He'd be an idiot to show his face anywhere near a Colton—especially since the family was littered with lawman types.

Jesse cleared his throat. "Sky, we're finished here. If your friend—"

"We're not friends exactly. More business acquaintances."

Studying her carefully, Jesse's eyes narrowed. "Any business I should know about?"

"Down boy. Don't make Dom defend himself. He's a doctor and needs his hands for surgery." She looked sadly at her brother. "But I have to go. It's time for me to get back to the store. And you have a plane to catch. I guess this is goodbye."

"Yeah." He pulled her into a bear hug. "Take care of yourself, sis. Stay out of trouble."

"You know me."

"Yeah. So I say again, stay out of trouble."

She laughed, then stepped away. "I love you. Take care."

"You, too. Don't worry about Kenny. We'll get him. Besides, he wouldn't dare show up around here. So you'll be safe in Black Arrow."

"I know." She kissed his cheek, then stepped out of the circle of his arms. "Say hi to Samantha for me. His new wife," she said to Dom.

At least someone managed to pull off a wedding, he thought.

"Congratulations." He held out his hand.

"Thanks," Jesse answered, squeezing his palm—hard.

Dom nodded. "Nice to meet you. All of you," he said, shaking hands all around.

"'Bye guys," Sky said, raising her hand in farewell as a chorus of deep voices responded.

Dom followed her outside where the cold Oklahoma day forced her to stop and put on her black coat. The sun was shining and the sky was blue, but the cold wind turned her cheeks and the tip of her cute turned-up nose red.

"How did you know where I was?" she asked, flipping up the collar of her coat.

"Your mom."

She nodded. "Of course. I don't even know why I asked. She fills in for me at the shop all the time. When I need backup."

Interesting choice of law enforcement lingo. But the majority of her family was in that line of work. "Can I buy you lunch?"

She shook her head. "I've already used up my lunch hour on family business."

"You wouldn't be trying to duck me, would you?"

"What was your first clue?"

"Since you're the boss, you should be able to take as much time off as you want. Especially with your mom as backup. You know. That whole force-of-nature thing you told me about. Seems to me your business is in good hands."

"Pretty good logic. But there's one flaw in your theory. What makes you think my mom doesn't have to be somewhere?"

"Does she?"

"No. She's a retired schoolteacher. And since my dad

retired from his security consulting business she's been looking for reasons to get out of the house. Too much togetherness, I suppose. But I don't want to take advantage. I told her I would be back in an hour."

He leaned a shoulder against the post holding up the sidewalk overhang. "There's this handy little invention. You may have heard of it. It's called a telephone. Many are portable and can be used from any location where there's cell reception."

"You're a real comedian," she said, but started laughing. "I have one of those handy, dandy gizmos. But I don't choose to use it. I choose to get back to work."

"So you *are* running away from me."

"That would be cowardly."

"If the shoe fits." He lifted one eyebrow. "Have you made up your mind yet? You said you'd sleep on it. Are you going to help me out?"

She turned worried gray eyes on him. "I think it's a bad idea, Dom."

"It's a good idea." He angled his chin toward the fire-damaged courthouse. "You said yourself that family sticks together."

She slung her purse strap over her shoulder. "Explain to me how deceiving your mother and grandmother is sticking together."

"It's for the greater good."

Equal parts of exhilaration and irritation coursed through him. Debating with her was more stimulating than anything he'd done in quite some time. Her gray eyes turned darker as anger swirled in their depths—like a stormy sky about to let loose. He found himself holding his breath in anticipation.

"It's a lie and that's wrong." She shook her head.

"No matter how you try to whitewash it, it's just plain dishonest. Truth, good—deceit, bad."

"That all depends on how you look at it." He shrugged. "I say they'll thank me for it."

"At the same time they're giving me the hate glare."

"You won't be around to see it." He felt a prick of something that could only be disappointment at the thought of her not being around, as in he wouldn't see her. "Look, Sky, bottom line, it would mean a lot to me if you would do this favor. I need an answer. Will you or won't you be my fiancée?"

As he asked the question, two older women walked by. They stared questioningly at Sky. She looked as though she wanted the earth to open up and swallow her. "Hi, Hazel. Hello, Ruthanne."

"Who's the handsome stranger?" the silver-haired woman asked.

"A friend," Sky answered. "Nice to see you both," she said as they continued down the sidewalk. When they were out of sight, she glared at him. "Now see what you've done? Those two are the biggest gossips in Black Arrow. In an hour, everyone in town will think I'm your fiancée."

"What a coincidence. I've got an engagement party that needs a fiancée. How about it?"

"Can we talk about this later? And privately?"

Alone with Sky was the best offer he'd had all day. "When and where?" he asked.

"My place—7:00 p.m."

Sky sat in her living room with Dom—déjà vu all over again. With one exception. This time she'd made the mistake of picking her favorite spot on the love seat first and he'd sat right beside her. In spite of the mouthwatering smell of chili simmering in a pot on the stove and corn bread baking in the oven, she could detect the fragrance of his cologne blending with the very male scent of his skin. Even to a girl who'd sworn off men, the effect sent a tidal wave of awareness rushing through her.

She leaned into her very own cushy corner of the love seat—as far from him as she could get without showing full retreat. "So tell me again. Why me? Besides the erroneous assumption that I owe you."

"Until I have time to find an appropriate wife, you'll do." He stretched his arm out along the sofa back.

"Be still my heart," she said, irritation not entirely canceling out the awareness she'd experienced just moments ago. "Well, you can take this pretense, Doctor, and shove it—"

He touched a finger to her lips. "Careful. Don't say anything you'll regret."

"Okay. You can take this pretense and shove it," she said again.

"Look, Sky. I don't have much time until my mother and grandmother arrive, expecting an engagement party. I have to be back at work seeing patients on Monday. I've got surgeries scheduled. There's no time to find someone else. My mother sacrificed everything for me."

"So did mine, but—"

He shook his head. "You don't understand. I saw her wear shoes with holes so big you could drive a Cadillac through. She patched her winter coat every year so she wouldn't have to buy another one. I remember nights when she wouldn't eat—claimed she wasn't hungry—so there would be enough food for me. But I knew she was lying. Things improved when she got a job as housekeeper to a wealthy family and I worked part-time. There was more money and she started to save for a trip. But then there were expenses for college, application fees, deposits, books.''

''But, Dom—''

He held his hand up. ''Don't interrupt. I'm on a roll. She went without clothes, food and fun. Then she said she couldn't travel until I was settled. Damn it. I was almost there.'' Wistfulness crept into his voice. ''I was engaged and she agreed to the trip. Finally, it was a chance to pamper her and have her slightest whim catered to. She won't do it if she thinks she's abandoning me.''

''You're a grown man living in a different state. How is that abandoning you?''

''I don't claim to understand how her mind works. I'm merely telling you what she says. But the bottom line is that I don't want her to give up, forego or go without ever again. Not because of me. And not if there's something I can do to prevent it.''

And he was nicknamed Dr. StoneHeart—why? Sky knew she would need a heart of stone to resist such a soul-baring speech. At best, her ticker was the consistency of melted marshmallow. Besides, she'd heard a man who was good to his mother was the best kind of husband material. Not that she cared since a husband was the last thing she wanted. That would take a relationship, a ship she had no intention of sailing on with a man who had found—then lost—Ms. Perfect.

''What about my business? Who's going to run it while I'm playing the doctor's fake fiancée?''

''Tell me your mother won't fill in for a short time.''

She sighed. ''I'm not a good liar. You said so yourself. That also means I won't be able to fool anyone.''

''Just do your best.''

"I'm going to hell." She met his gaze. "And so are you—encouraging me to lie," she said, shaking her head.

"Is that a yes?"

"No. That was, we both know I have nothing to feel guilty about. And if I do this for you, maybe you should return the favor."

"Pretend to be your fiancée?"

She smiled. "No. What are you going to do for me?"

"I already promised to pay for the rings. What more do you want?" he asked, lifting one eyebrow.

She considered the question for several moments. "I can't think of a blessed thing. Can I have a favor rain check?"

"As soon as you figure something out, you got it." He met her gaze. "Now, is it a yes?"

She nodded. "Yes."

"I could hug you."

She held up her hand. "I'd rather you didn't."

"Your wish is my command." Instead he brushed a fingertip over her cheekbone. "I don't know how to thank you."

"You thanked your mom with a cruise," she said, giving him her most hopeful look.

"Nice try."

"It was worth a shot." She tapped her finger against her lip thoughtfully. "Now back to the problem. Fibs work best if you weave enough of the truth in to sound convincing."

"For someone who's not very good at this, you seem quite knowledgeable about the technique."

"Nothing more than common sense. But seriously, we need to exchange some information about ourselves to pull this off."

"Like what?"

She thought for a minute. "First of all, how did we meet?"

"I came to Black Arrow to settle the bill for wedding rings."

"Not you and me. You and Shelby."

"She lives in Midland where her father's oil business is located. But she came to see me as a patient."

"I'm not geographically gifted, but there's a lot of miles between the two cities. Why Houston?"

"She'd heard about my reputation as a plastic surgeon and wanted a consultation. Thanksgiving weekend she made the trip in the limo."

"Limo? She must have something against flying."

"Hates it."

"Did it ever occur to you she was spending an excessive amount of time with the chauffeur?"

"Hindsight is twenty-twenty," he answered ruefully. "Her life will be one long road trip."

"If memory serves, Shelby looked perfect to me. What part did she want you to fix? Nose? Breasts? Chin? Eyelids? Ears?"

"Uh-uh," he said, shaking his head. "I can't discuss that. Patient confidentiality."

"Okay." It didn't matter anyway. But she couldn't decide whether or not she envied the woman who could, without a whole lot of consideration, take the steps to alter her appearance. Then she did the math on the length of his acquaintance with his bride-to-be and whistled admiringly. "Thanksgiving? Fast work, Doc."

"As you pointed out, I don't have a lot of time to waste. Besides, when it's right, you just go for it."

Guilt hit her again. "I'm sorry things didn't work out between you and Shelby."

"Me, too," he said, his tone sharp, clipped. "But what's that saying about spilled milk? Let's get back to business."

"Okay," she said, not wanting to think too much about her part in it. "You know, I just thought of a problem." One of many, but who was keeping score? "I don't look anything like Shelby. She has blond hair and blue eyes and I...don't. How are you going to explain that? I know you're a plastic surgeon, but even you're not that good. Or that fast."

"I've given the matter some thought and it's not a problem. First, the invitations haven't gone out yet. I'll pull the ones going to her friends and family. No one at the party will recognize her."

"What about your friends?"

"They know I'm involved with someone, but no one has met her."

"No one? Not your friends or the people you work with? Did you keep her in a closet?" When he made a dismissive noise, she continued. "I don't get it. You dated. You asked her to marry you. How come your acquaintances haven't met the woman you love?"

"As you pointed out, I'm a fast worker." He shifted uncomfortably then scowled at her. "It was a whirlwind courtship, one she insisted on keeping secret. If the tabloids got wind of it, she assured me I would have no peace. I couldn't chance my work being disrupted or my patients compromised by that kind of publicity."

Sky couldn't help thinking that if she were engaged to Dom for real, she would take out an ad in every newspaper in town. Including tabloids that wouldn't give two hoots about her, because she wasn't a rich socialite.

"Shelby got this crazy idea to have a surprise party. When everyone showed up, she wanted to tell them in person to see the look on their faces. Only my mother and grandmother know we planned to announce the engagement.''

''Did it ever occur to you that Shelby is a little—''

''What?''

''Flaky,'' she said hesitantly. ''Flighty? No pun intended, especially since she won't step foot in a plane.''

''No. In my opinion she's free-spirited, aggressive and independent.''

''Okay.''

''Because of her free-spirited party planning, there's no problem with you impersonating Shelby,'' he finished. ''I'll mail the invitations first thing when I get back. The guests should get them with about three weeks' notice. A little fast, but this is all for my mother's benefit, anyway. Like I said, no problem.''

None, other than disregarding her own moral code.

Sky eyed him critically. ''Does your mother know what an expert schemer you are?''

''Actually, I'm not. The circumstances just presented themselves and I'm going with it.''

''A schemer by any other name—''

He gently tapped her nose. ''If you tell her, I'll…''

''You know a threat only works if you finish it. However, I think I've got the upper hand here. You're the one with the secret. I'm only the hired muscle, helping you pull it off.''

He scowled and she knew she had him. ''Doctor, does that expression frighten women and small children?''

''Yes. Not to mention hospital personnel and my office staff.''

''I'm not intimidated.''

He took a lock of her hair between his thumb and

forefinger and rubbed it. "Has anyone ever told you your hair is like silk?"

"No. And, moving right along..." she said, her heart pounding. "I don't think I can just step into the role of your fiancée blind. I probably should have some information about her. Not to mention that I should know some basic facts about you."

"Probably a good idea."

"I think so. And on that note, let the information dump begin. What's your favorite color?"

"Blue. Yours?"

"Green," she answered automatically. Then she shook her head. "But that's useless information. What color does Shelby like?"

"I don't know if she ever mentioned it. Is that important?"

"I suppose not. If there won't be anyone there who knows her. For the record, she likes red."

"How do you know?" he asked.

"When we were going over designs for the rings, she toyed with the idea of using rubies because they're her favorite color. I can't believe you didn't know that. The color a person is drawn to says a lot about who they are."

"Hmm." He met her gaze. "What does green say about you?"

"I'm serene and easygoing. I don't like conflict or unnecessary stress cluttering up my life. But enough about me," she said before he could challenge her. "Back to basics. Where were you born?"

"California. Mom still lives there."

"You mean she lives halfway across the country from you and still feels that taking a cruise is equivalent to abandoning you?"

"Since I can't explain the twists and turns of the maternal mind, I suggest we move on. I graduated from U.C.L.A. and went to medical school in Texas. What about you?"

"I was born in Germany. My dad was in the army and we traveled around a lot. He was discharged when I was three and that's when we settled in Black Arrow. So he could be near his family."

"So you're an army brat?"

"I've never been a brat in my life." Darn, she'd done it again, answered as herself. "Where was Shelby born and raised?"

"Midland. She went to Yale and graduated with a degree in theater. About as useful as a—"

"Degree in fine arts? That's what I studied," she said. The revelation brought up all the disturbing memories of the time when she'd had to justify her chosen course of study to a family who didn't understand. If she'd needed it, that was more proof she didn't fit in. "It comes in handy if one has a keen interest in jewelry design instead of law enforcement."

"I sense some defensiveness."

"You're imagining it. Besides, we don't need to talk about me. I need all the info on Shelby I can get. Actually, I could use a couple of her acting classes."

"Don't worry. This is going to be a piece of cake, Sky. We merely have to pretend to be an engaged couple. You just have to be yourself. No one knows Shelby."

Not even you, she thought. "Okay. But that brings up another problem."

"Being yourself?" he asked frowning.

"No. Acting like an engaged couple. We met yesterday. We're going to have to be practically joined at the hip. What if I can't pretend to be attracted? Not that you're a troll or anything, but—''

''Thanks, I think,'' he said, his dark eyes gleaming with amusement. But he didn't smile. And something dangerous joined the humor glimmering in his gaze.

''You know what I mean. A man and a woman become a couple because of chemistry. What if we have to kiss? What if I can't pull it off?''

''Don't you think you're selling me short?''

''How?''

''Kissing is all about technique.''

''Maybe, but what if we're forced into a situation and you kiss me or I kiss you and one of us gags or something—'' She sighed.

''How high are your standards?'' he asked.

''What I'm trying to say is, we don't want any surprises. I don't want to go into this cold.''

''You know what? You're right.''

Before Sky knew what was happening, he leaned over, put his hands at her waist, and slid her onto his lap. She was staring into blue eyes that suddenly smoldered like hot coals.

''A fiancée would put her arms around me.'' His voice was husky, deep, a seductive drawl.

''R-right.''

But she couldn't move, so he lifted first one arm then the other onto his broad shoulders. With a satisfied expression on his face, he settled his hands loosely at her waist. Awkward didn't come close to describing how she felt, but he looked completely comfortable. Completely male. Exceptionally sexy. Enormously appealing. Her heart pounded to beat the band and she couldn't seem to take in a deep breath.

The intense look in his eyes made her skin tingle and her pulse pound. Why him? Why her? Why now?

"Loosen up," he ordered. "You're stiff as a board."

"See? What if this happened in front of your friends? Doing it cold—"

Suddenly he lowered his head and touched his lips to hers. In a heartbeat, talking was the last thing she wanted to do.

Chapter Four

As Dom slowly and deliberately savored her incredibly soft lips, he wondered which god he'd pleased and how to do it again. He barely knew Sky, but visions of her had kept him awake long into the night. Now here he was, kissing this amazingly sensuous woman. And enjoying it far more than he should. But how could that be? Until a short time ago, he'd been engaged to Shelby. Suddenly everything was too tight: his conscience, his chest, his breathing and his jeans.

This reaction *had* to be about missing his fiancée. Actions this crazy were surely a direct result of the anger, disappointment and, yes, the hit his pride had taken after her note revealed he'd lost her to the chauffeur. His instant, intense attraction to Sky had to be as simple and as complicated as that. Because this was only the fourth time he'd seen Sky Colton in barely twenty-four hours.

She was still wearing the clingy cream sweater and long, slim wool skirt from earlier that day when he'd thought her so feminine, sophisticated, refined and sexy as hell. But her ensemble, even with her in it, wouldn't account for him having the hots like this unless it was motivated by some whacked-out, delayed response to rejection. However, if he'd known earlier today how good her shapely little bottom would feel in his lap, her male relatives, teeming with testosterone, would have had a thing or two to say and three hundred things to do to him.

He needed to slow things down. Breaking the kiss, he inhaled deeply, then let the breath out slowly. As he glanced down, he noticed she'd kicked off her high heels. Her nylon-clad ankles and lower calves were visible below the hem of her skirt and brushed against his leg with a subtle, erotic whisper. Even through his jeans, the contact was electric.

Sucking in a breath, he swung his gaze back to her face. Her eyes were wide with wonder, her kiss-swollen lips parted, her respirations quick and uneven. Diagnosis: he wanted her—bad.

This was all about getting comfortable with her, he reminded himself. But not *that* comfortable. They were two of the stooges in a Three Stooges farce. This was part of a ruse to achieve a goal. Nothing more. But, man, she packed a powerful punch. Was she that good an actress? Or—

No, he wasn't going there. Been down that rut-filled road all too recently. He would just chalk it up to the fact that his leading lady in this parody slipped seamlessly into the role, making it easy for him to pretend she was the woman he wanted to marry. But a respected doctor didn't do things like this. Unless the woman had bewitched him.

"Dom—"

The sound of his name spoken in her breathless voice

did insane things to his own pulse and respirations. But somehow he managed to say, "What?"

She took in air. "I think that kiss answers my question."

"Which one?" he asked, his consciousness empty of everything but her. Then a sliver of sanity returned. "You mean, about whether or not we can be convincing as an about-to-be-married couple?"

"That would be the one. You can let me go now," she said, halfheartedly nudging his shoulder.

"My mom is no fool and she knows me pretty well. If we're not convincing, she'll see through the whole scheme. Don't you think we could use a little more practice?"

Why had he suggested that? Apparently his mind and body had been taken over by aliens. It was the only explanation.

"Practice makes perfect. Or so I've heard. I guess a little more couldn't hurt." She ran her tongue across her full upper lip.

The sight of her, doing that, drove him wild and he was beyond analyzing, diagnosing or caring why. He lowered his head and with an effort, he kept his mouth gentle on hers when every male instinct he possessed urged him to lay claim to her. He scattered light kisses on her lips as he wrapped his arms around her, pulling her more securely against his chest. Her arms tightened around his neck and her sweet breath whispered across his cheek.

Shifting his position on the love seat, he leaned her back, cushioning her in the bend of his arm. He hovered over her, marveling at how perfect she fit against him. She was exquisitely soft and smelled like flowers. He identified the expression of amazement in her big, beautiful gray eyes and realized he shared the sensation, but he had more important things to do than puzzle out the feelings. He *had* to brush his knuckle across her cheek.

"Yup," he said.

"What?"

"Your skin is just as soft as it looks."

"The miracle of cold cream. And washing my face every night without fail. Do you know what happens to your skin if you sleep in your makeup? Of course you wouldn't. You're a man—who's not a dermatologist—"

He pressed a finger to her lips. "You're babbling. Do I make you nervous?"

She shook her head, but her eyes were still wide.

"Don't be. We're in this together," he said, hearing the husky tone of his voice as he tunneled his fingers into her hair.

The strands *were* like silk. But if he told her so again, it might crank up her nerves even more. That was something he didn't want to do. There was something he *did* want to do, and he wanted it more than his next breath.

Dom ran his tongue along her top lip, then traced the bottom one until she opened for him. Dipping inside, he stroked a trail across the roof of her mouth. A thrill of satisfaction rippled through him when she shivered delicately, then strained toward him.

Rational thought disappeared as she gently touched the tip of her tongue to the roof of his mouth, mirroring what he'd just done to her. Hot blood raced through him, fast and furious. It made him light-headed and pounded in his ears, then quickly descended to points south. Their tongues dueled in a fierce, demanding dance.

His breath came faster and his skin felt too tight. He retreated from her lips to nibble kisses from the corner of her mouth and across her cheek. Stopping momentarily to tease her earlobe, he caught it between his teeth and toyed gently until he heard her moan with pleasure.

He moved to a spot just a little lower, focusing his attention on her neck. He kissed her there, sucking gently, followed by a soft touch with his tongue. She trembled and gasped breathlessly. Her chest rose and fell rapidly as she squirmed against him, tightening her already firm grip on his neck. Her sexy little movements, the passionate noises she made, set his body on fire—

Suddenly a noise like an airhorn filled the apartment. Sky went stiff, then sat up out of the circle of his arms.

Eyes glazed with passion, she looked around. Then she gasped and jumped off his lap. "We're on fire! Look at the smoke. What the— Good grief. I forgot the cornbread!"

She raced into the kitchen and he followed, stopping to open windows and fan the smoke out. She yanked the oven door almost off its hinges. Using a mitt, she pulled out the smoldering baking dish and set it on top of one of the cold burners. Then she grabbed a chair, climbed up on it and pressed the button to turn off the alarm.

Adding to the confusion, the telephone rang. She jumped down and answered it, "False alarm."

Dom figured she must have the smoke detector and security system wired together and monitored.

"No." She brushed the hair out of her eyes. "Something's actually burning. But, really, everything's fine. I've got it under control. Okay. Thanks."

He watched Sky hang up the phone. She took the oven mitt and fanned the smoke toward the open window.

After huffing out a breath of air, she said, "That scared the heck out of me. My adrenaline is pumping, how about yours?"

"Yeah." He was pumped all right, full of testosterone, with a healthy dose of frustration thrown in.

"Dress rehearsal went well. Don't you think?" she asked shakily. "I didn't gag."

"There's an endorsement," he said ruefully.

"I just have one thing to say. Why the heck did that StoneHeart nickname stick?"

He ran his fingers through his hair. "Beats me. I certainly don't get the relevance."

"I'm not sure if it's relevant, but I'm not cold anymore."

That makes two of us, he thought. He'd never lost himself so completely while kissing a woman. He'd never—

Never? Definitely never. He'd been so focused on Sky, how good it felt to hold her, how much he enjoyed kissing her, that he'd been oblivious to everything. That had never happened to him before. Not even with his bride-to-be. He'd never been so completely caught up in kissing Shelby that he'd forgotten where he was. He'd never been strung so tight that he'd have been unaware of a room full of smoke.

What was that all about?

Based on his recent romantic track record, instinct told him to hit the ground running—as far and as fast as he could away from Sky Colton. Unfortunately he had a plan that meant more to him than his own peace of mind and he needed her to help him carry it out.

In the luxury SUV, Sky glanced over at Dom in the driver's seat. He had a nice profile, she decided. She figured if Dom doctored a fraction as skillfully as he kissed, he could come darn close to healing the dead. She wondered if he transmitted some sort of electrical energy that scrambled her brain waves. It was as plausible as any other explanation for why she'd been oblivious to smoke billowing through her apartment. Faulty brain function would also account for the fact that she was now in Houston and how it had happened so fast.

This was Sunday—two days after meeting him. She felt as if she'd been caught in some weird sci-fi scenario, that time had flung her forward like a slingshot. On the other hand, it seemed as if she'd known him forever. But when she did the math, they were still practically strangers.

Dom had changed his flight out of the local airport to a later one and booked her on it, as well. She'd needed the extra time to make business and personal preparations for her absence.

"Tell me again why I had to accompany you back to Houston today for a party that's several weeks away."

He glanced at her, but she couldn't read his expression in the dark. "You need time to acclimate to your surroundings."

"Uh-huh."

"Since Shelby doesn't live in Houston, you don't have to know much about the city itself. But she's spent time with me here, so you'll need to cultivate a certain comfort level."

"Comfort," she repeated nodding her head. "Yeah. Like that's going to happen. What planet are you from?"

A passing streetlight illuminated his bemused expression. "Are you always this cranky after you get off a plane?"

"This isn't cranky. If you stick around long enough I'll show you cranky." She twisted her fingers together in her lap. "I should warn you. Bram was not happy about this."

"Oh?"

"Oh, nothing. He told me what Great-Grandpa George WhiteBear said."

"Which was?"

"He insisted that danger lurks in the big city. And it's always darkest just before the dawn. Go ahead and laugh, but his insights have an uncanny way of proving true."

"I'm not laughing. But I would like to point out that it doesn't take second sight, mystical abilities or psychic inclinations to come up with that."

"He ran a background check on you."

"Grandpa George?"

"No. Bram. You're squeaky clean. Everything checks out." She looked out the window as they exited the freeway. "But that doesn't mean he approves of what I'm doing. He said if you even sneeze funny, he'll mobilize the lawman types so fast it will make your head spin."

Dom glanced at her. "Did you tell him what you're doing?"

"Voluntarily confess to the sheriff that I'm committing fraud? Isn't that what it's called when you impersonate someone? Of course I didn't tell him. Do I have *felon* written on my forehead?" She sighed. "I told him I was going on a buying trip, that there was a gem show in Houston I wanted to check out, and that I was also considering opening a branch of my business in the city."

"Then why did he check me out?"

"Because I'm a bad liar. He figured out that my trip has something to do with you. 'O what a tangled web we weave when first we practice to deceive.' Good Lord, I'm starting to spout platitudes like my great-grandpa George."

"So he didn't buy it?"

"Grandpa George?"

"No," he said, his tone brimming with humor. "The sheriff. And he didn't stop you."

"I'm over twenty-one."

"How much over?"

"Five years." Sky thought she heard a low groan from his side of the car, but figured her ears were still plugged from the flight. "And since I am an adult, there was no way short of locking me up that he could stop me. On the upside, my mother likes you."

"There's something."

"Yeah. She and my dad are having some issues since he retired—basically because he's around all the time without much to do. That's why she thought it would be good for her to sub for me at the jewelry shop. Anyway, if she needs anything, she can get in touch with me by cell phone or e-mail. But traditionally January is a pretty slow retail month."

"Isn't the timing of my misfortune fortuitous?" he asked, irony lacing his words.

She glanced at him. Light from the stores along the street created shadows that danced across his face. That made it impossible to read his expression. "Sorry. I didn't mean it that way. No offense."

"None taken."

Really? He loved Shelby and he would never be with her. She knew how painful that situation could be. She'd loved the man she was going to marry. When she'd figured out that he had wanted her to be something she wasn't, she'd had to stop the ceremony. That didn't mean she'd stopped loving him. Misery and sadness had been her new best friends for a while.

Having heartache as her constant companion had

made her empathetic. She tried her best not to deliberately hurt other people. But she kept forgetting how badly Dom must be feeling. If she had to guess, she'd say that was because of the way he'd kissed her. He was a spurned lover, yet he'd made her feel as though she were the only woman in the world. How did he do that?

Wrapped up tightly in her own thoughts, Sky hadn't noticed right away that they were driving through a private neighborhood. A very well-to-do neighborhood by the size of the homes. Dom made several turns, then pulled into a long driveway with a very large brick house to the right of it. Strategically placed lights surrounded the structure.

"You live in that château?" she asked, cocking her thumb in its direction.

"Be it ever so humble." He shrugged.

"What are we doing here? I thought you were taking me to a hotel."

"When we talked about making you comfortable in this scenario, that sort of implied my place."

"Not to me. I figured it meant field trips. During daylight hours," she added, hating that she sounded like a prissy spinster. She wasn't. Prissy, that is. Because she couldn't deny that she was still a single woman. Almost married didn't count.

"Aren't you tired, Sky? And hungry? Can we talk about this inside?" He opened his door and stepped out.

She'd lost her appetite, but she knew for a fact she wasn't a prude. In the matters of men and women, she believed in letting nature take its course. She made no judgments about a couple cohabiting before marriage. It was no big deal. But—wow! Here they were at his place and it suddenly felt like a big deal. If they'd never kissed, would she be so skittish about this? The easy answer was no. If he'd never kissed her the way he had, living here with him for a couple of weeks wouldn't rate a second thought.

But now she most certainly had thoughts—second, third and fourth ones. Why did it make her nervous? Because something might happen? She scoffed at the idea. Then she remembered the intoxicating sensation of his mouth on hers, the strength and security of his arms around her, the way he'd heated her from head to toe with just the right touch here and a whisper of a caress there. Uh-oh.

She was so in trouble here.

If only she'd had time to give more consideration to what getting comfortable with her surroundings meant. He opened the passenger door and held out his hand to help her down. Now he had to go and be a gentleman on top of being the best kisser she'd ever made out with.

She sighed as she braced herself for the electricity that always happened when he touched her. Then she put her hand in his and slid down. "Thanks."

"You're welcome."

He walked to the back of the SUV and opened the hatch to retrieve her suitcase, garment bag and overnight case along with his one small carry-on. Between the two of them, they carted it all to the house. He unlocked the door and swung it wide before they set everything on the wooden floor just inside. Reaching over, he flipped several switches and the interior of the house lit up.

Very nice, Sky thought. Granted, she was no stranger to opulence, considering what she did for a living. But he was a bachelor. She wasn't sure what she'd expected, but certainly not this. It was beautiful.

"Wow," she said. "Who keeps these wood floors so clean you can eat off them?"

"I have a service," he answered, setting his keys on a credenza just inside the door. It looked old, not old bad, but old antique and in very nice shape. A lovely, graceful mahogany piece.

The open floor plan seemed to go on and on and on. As she moved farther inside, she could see the living room to her left, and right was the dining area with the family room straight ahead. It looked as if the whole downstairs was wood floor with strategically placed and very expensive area rugs.

Two large overstuffed, off-white sofas faced each other in front of the living room fireplace. On either side of it, built-in shelves stuffed with books filled the space from the floor to the twelve-foot ceiling. In the corner was a shined-to-perfection baby grand piano while occasional tables were placed throughout the room. The walls were painted a beige color, the shade of heavily creamed coffee. White baseboards, chair rail and crown molding contrasted beautifully and matching shutters covered the windows.

"Would you like a guided tour?" he asked.

"Very much. If I take the self-guided one, I might never be heard from again. This is a lot of house for one person."

When he stared at the openness with a bleak expression, Sky could have bitten her tongue. It seemed every time she opened her mouth, she was reminding him that he'd been dumped. But his face—that wonderful face with character lines in all the right places—if she had to describe it, *lonely* was the first word that came to mind. Sad, too. Either or both emotions tugged at her heart. This was where he'd expected to bring his bride and start a life. Instead he'd brought her—a stand-in, phony, fake, place-holder.

Guilt, her constant companion since meeting him, dropped like a stone on her chest. She was glad she'd agreed to help him out of his predicament. At least he wouldn't be completely alone for a little while. Maybe by the time she went back to Black Arrow, his pain and loneliness would be a bit less, or at least a tad easier to bear.

But what about this strange attraction she felt for him? It complicated the agreement she'd made to impersonate his fiancée. But that particular problem was hers. She owned it and he need never know how she felt. A few weeks from now their bargain would be history anyway.

In the meantime she wanted to see his house. "Lead on, Dr. Do Right."

He looked down at her and one dark eyebrow rose, but his dark expression didn't ease much. "Excuse me?"

"Don't ask. You be the general, I'll be the troops."

"Does that mean you follow orders?"

Without answering, she breezed by him, close enough to breathe in the tantalizing scent of his skin. Her mistake, she realized when her heart fluttered. In a house with this much square footage, there was ample room to allow a safe distance between them. But no. Calamity Colton just barreled straight ahead without a thought to her warnings or resolves. The story of her life, she thought with a sigh.

"Something wrong?" He held up his hand. "Never mind. It's obvious. You have a problem following orders."

"Doctor's orders?"

"Any orders."

"We'll see, won't we." She shrugged. "I would really like to see the kitchen."

"This way," he said, extending his arm.

She followed him into the family room that connected to the kitchen. A bank of white-painted French doors with arches above revealed the brick patio and pool area beyond. The yard was bathed in light from spotlights liberally placed around the perimeter. Another fireplace, this one see-through with openings on both sides, graced the wall between the two rooms. Sky walked into the kitchen and groaned.

"Now what's wrong?"

"Nothing. That sound you heard was envy spilling over. Any cook worth his or her salt would love this room," she said, trying to take everything in.

A huge refrigerator stood proudly between the built-in oven and microwave. Light wood cabinetry brightened the cupboards and seemed to invite her to stay. A center island, its marbled countertop speckled in shades of brown, beige and cream, dominated the center of the work area. A cooktop separated the kitchen from the family room. This was a great setup for entertaining, she thought. The openness allowed the chef to be a part of any festivities and to see through the French doors and into the backyard.

"Wow," she said again. "I'm speechless. The place just gets better and better."

"Wait till you see the bedroom."

"*The* bedroom?" Please, she silently begged, don't let him notice that my cheeks are as hot as the face of the sun. "Surely a house the size of a hotel has more than one."

"Six. But the master is great. This way," he said, leading her back the way they'd come.

The master bedroom was also on the first floor, at the back of the house. He flipped a switch and the lamps on either side of the bed lit up. She stepped onto light beige carpet and felt as if she'd sunk up to her knees. The mattress was king-size and framed by a brass headboard and footboard. It was completely lovely and like nothing she'd ever seen in the stores.

Reverently touching one of the thick posts she asked, "Is this an antique?"

He nodded. "I found it in Fredricksburg. As near as I've been able to determine, it's late nineteenth century."

"Wow. It's wonderful."

"I like it," he said, with a hint of something in his voice, as if he was defending his choice. "The dressing area is around the corner." He flipped another switch and she walked into a brightly lit area with mirrors on three sides.

"A girl could see every flaw in here," she commented.

"If she had any. But you've got nothing to worry about." He met her gaze in the mirror and the intensity in his eyes caused her heart to trip. He pointed to a door. "Tub and shower are through there."

"What's upstairs?"

"Game room with pool table and dartboard. And five bedrooms."

"So I can have my pick?" she asked, folding her arms over her chest as she leaned back against the vanity with double sinks.

One corner of his mouth curved up. "So you changed your mind about wanting to go to a hotel?"

"That was before I knew this place was as *big* as a hotel." Distracted by the attractive yet comfortable surroundings, she continued. "There's plenty of room. You won't get under my skin—"

"Is that so?"

"I meant, underfoot. On each other's nerves. Surely with all this room, we can live together without violating each other's space." The gleam stealing into his eyes made her the tiniest bit uneasy.

"I'm sure you're right. And to answer your question, you're welcome to pick a bedroom. At least until my mother and grandmother arrive."

"Of course," she said. "I won't get too comfortable. Maybe your mother or grandmother will want the room I choose and I'll have to move."

"There's no maybe about it."

"How's that?" she asked.

"You'll definitely have to change rooms."

She hoped he meant that his relatives had visited before and already staked claims to specific sleeping quarters. But something about the expression on his face and the look in his eyes told her she would be wrong.

"What does that mean?"

"You'll definitely have to move. Into the master bedroom," he added.

"I see," she answered as calmly as she could. "And will you be moving, also?"

"Yes."

"Okay." She permitted herself a small sigh of relief.

"I'll be moving over to make room for you in the bed."

Chapter Five

"Make room for me in *your* bed?" Sky asked, incredulous.

"Yes."

Dom hummed with anticipation. He felt a debate coming on and couldn't stop the zing of exhilaration that arced through him.

She straightened away from the vanity. In the mirror he could see the back of her shiny, dark hair skim her slender shoulders, just above her trim back. She wore a red pullover sweater and jeans that hugged all her curves. But it was her gray eyes, flashing like molten silver, that told him she had one or two things to say. When she turned and showed him her back for real, then walked from the room, he was surprised.

"Sky?"

He couldn't claim to know her well, but he would bet his favorite stethoscope it wasn't normal for her to walk away without a single verbal shot fired. He followed her to the kitchen.

"Sky?"

She'd opened the refrigerator and glanced at him over her shoulder. "I hope you don't mind."

He shrugged. "Of course not. I expect you to make yourself at home. Getting comfortable here is what this is all about."

"So you said. And you're certainly doing everything possible to make that happen," she added. She pulled out a carton of eggs, cheese and some mushrooms, setting them on the counter. "What with moving me into your bed and all."

"There's a reason for that."

"Of course there is." Her voice dripped sarcasm. Obviously she didn't believe him.

She found a bowl and picked up an egg, whacking it so hard against the rim, it disintegrated inside—sliming down the side.

Dom leaned his elbows on the center work island. He watched her back, hoping she would bend over. It was a sight for sore eyes, he remembered. The first night he'd met her—was it only a couple of days ago?—she'd bent to look into her refrigerator, giving him an unrestricted view. Her derriere was a work of art and he would bet she'd never had it worked on surgically. But this time she didn't bend over. In fact, he wondered if she could bend at all, stiff as she was. She poured the gunky mess into the garbage disposal and rinsed out the bowl, then set it back on the counter.

"You think I have an ulterior motive?" he asked.

Over her shoulder she slid him a wry look. "You're a guy. You can't help it. That doesn't mean I need to make this easy for you."

"You know, Sky, coming from a law-enforcement family like you do has given you a suspicious mind. Not only that, you're cynical. Assume the worst first, ask questions later."

"I didn't ask questions," she pointed out. "That was my mistake." She cracked several eggs successfully into the bowl, then started to cut up mushrooms.

He wondered if he should worry about having this discussion/debate with her while she was wielding a knife. "At the risk of irritating you, I'd like to point out that you did ask a question. You wanted to know if I was making room in my bed for you. And the answer was yes."

"And you said there's a good reason. I'm waiting in a heightened state of anticipation to hear what it is."

"Actually I said I had a reason. You need to decide whether or not it's a good one."

She turned toward him, leaving the island between them. Setting her hands on the top she asked, "Are you going to split hairs all night, or are you going to share the reason with me?"

"It's quite simple really, and central to this plan being successful. My mother knows that Shelby moved in with me."

Dom watched her eyes. The molten-silver look cooled, leaving behind an expression that reminded him of storm clouds waiting to spill snow. This wasn't the best time to think she was the most beautiful woman he'd ever seen. And he figured it was a worse time to say it. As a kid he'd been in enough fights to learn you waited for your opponent to make a move, then you put up a defense.

"When did Shelby move in?"

"After I asked her to marry me. Around the holidays."

"And your mother knows?" she asked doubtfully.

"I got her and my grandmother computers the Christmas before last. We communicate every week either through e-mail or phone calls."

"And you thought you needed to share the fact that a woman you weren't married to had taken up residence in your home?"

"We were engaged at the time. It was news I knew would make my mother happy."

"So you volunteered the information that Shelby was sharing your bed?"

"Of course not. Guys don't tell their mothers stuff like that."

"Then there's no reason for me to change rooms."

"Yes, there is. Given the fact that Shelby and I were planning to be married, not to mention that this is a new millennium and my mother wasn't born yesterday, she figured out all by herself that I didn't put my fiancée in the guest room."

Dom watched a pink color brush over Sky's cheeks. He would swear it wasn't from embarrassment. He didn't think it was from anger, either. What emotion was left? Jealousy? He scoffed. If Sky had any feelings like that for him, he wouldn't have had to work so hard to get her here. Unless she was attracted to him and fighting the feelings.

She turned away from him and rooted through the kitchen drawers for something.

"What do you need?" he asked.

"A grater."

"Are you planning to use it on me?"

That earned him a hooded look. "Why would I do that?"

"You look angry enough to skin me alive."

One corner of her mouth turned up. "I am. But if I

was planning to do you physical harm, it wouldn't be with a cheese grater."

"Oh? What would be your weapon of choice? A rolling pin?"

"Nope. A spoon."

She was something. He never knew what she would say next. "Why a spoon? Or I guess the question should be—what would you do with it?"

"I'd cut your heart out. And before you ask, I would use a spoon because it would hurt more."

"And why would you want to hurt me?"

She faced him full-on, her hands on her hips. "Okay, Dr. Dense, here it is. I'm annoyed that you didn't give me this information before I turned my life upside down and left Black Arrow."

"Would it have made a difference?"

"You bet your digital thermometer it would."

"Why?"

"One wonders how you ever managed to get through college, let alone medical school. I'll spell it out for you. It's not wise to share a man's bed if you've never been out on a date with him."

"So no one has ever swept you off your feet?"

"Once." She looked down. "But we're not talking about me. This is about you keeping important facts from me that I needed to make an informed decision."

"I don't see why it's a big deal. The plan is still the same. Convince my mother and grandmother that we're planning to be married. Get them on the cruise." He shrugged. "You go your way, I go mine. And you've redeemed yourself for breaking up my happy home."

"I thought that home-wrecker thing was you being overly dramatic. I agreed to this charade before I knew you and Shelby were playing house together."

"Okay. I'll come clean. I didn't tell you because I was afraid of this reaction." Normally he was a "truth, the whole truth and nothing but the truth" kind of guy. But he'd kept this part from her because he was afraid she would have refused to help him. Only now did he realize how very much he had wanted her there. "I needed you and I was concerned that if you knew it meant sharing a room, you might back out."

"Darn right."

"It's no big deal, Sky. You take one of the upstairs rooms until my family arrives. Then we'll share my room. They'll be here for a couple days, until the party. The next day they leave. We'll be like brother and sister."

She shook her head at him as if he didn't have a clue. "I'll go through with this because a Colton doesn't go back on a promise. At least not without a good reason," she added. "And I don't have one. Because you're right. Sharing a room with you is no big deal." She lifted her chin as if she expected him to argue her point.

"I knew you were sensible."

"You thought I was a brainless bimbo who sold jewelry and dispensed thoughtless advice that wrecked homes."

"I don't anymore."

And that was the hell of it. He'd discovered she was smart, funny and kept him on his toes. Worse, he liked her, liked spending time with her. That was far more dangerous than he would have imagined.

Sky found the number of Dom's suite in the medical office building next to the hospital. She checked the name on the door just to be sure. Dominic Rodriguez, M.D. Yup, this was the right place. She went inside and glanced around. Not a single patient to be seen. Good. She'd timed her errand perfectly.

Every overstuffed chair and leather couch in the large, comfortably furnished waiting area was empty. The room was decorated in shades of mauve, light green and powder blue. Serviceable carpet covered the floor in a calming shade of celery-green. Framed prints hung on the walls; some, colorful oils, others enlarged black-and-whites of ocean and beach scenes.

She walked up to the reception counter and lifted her hand to knock on the sliding-glass window. Muted voices carried to her from the other side of the glass. Suddenly the door to the right of the counter opened and two women walked through. Sky judged them to be mother and teenage daughter.

The girl said, "Mom, can we go to the mall later? I want to get a really short skirt to wear to the party Friday night."

"Okay." The older woman noticed Sky watching and beamed at her. "I'm not usually so permissive. Normally I would go to the mat in refusing her a request like that. But after what we've been through, I would give her just about anything."

"Really?" Sky asked.

The woman nodded. "There was an accident in Kate's chemistry class. Chemicals, a Bunsen burner, a hyper kid doing something stupid. Anyway, her arms and legs were badly burned. She felt so hideously scarred, she swore she'd wear a suit of armor if I made her go out in public. Fortunately, Dr. Rodriguez is a plastic surgeon who specializes in burn cases. He treated her in the emergency room and has supervised her treatment ever since. He's a miracle worker."

"Is that so?"

"I know that's more than you probably wanted to know, but I thought it might help to ease your mind. Since you're waiting to see him." She tapped her lip. "And something else that will make you feel better as a patient. The nurses in the hospital are scared to death of him."

Sky blinked. "Why would that reassure me?"

"When Kate was in the hospital he was so good with her. But if any of the patient care staff so much as changed a bandage wrong, he would excuse himself and find out who was responsible. He wants perfection for his patients."

"He's so cool," Kate said. "And cute for an older guy."

"Yeah," Sky said wryly. She'd noticed. There was no point in telling them she wasn't there as a patient. But she was curious about the teen's treatment. "So what did he do?"

"The burned areas had to be covered to heal," the teen said. "The doctor used some donated skin, kind of like blood transfusions, only it was skin. I know it sounds gross, but he said it makes all the difference. And he was right. As the burns healed and the covering was rejected, the doctor grafted some of my own skin over the scars. Now you can barely see where the burns were. I never thought I'd be able to wear a short skirt or sleeveless blouse again. Especially not a strapless dress to the winter formal," she gushed.

"But you are?" Sky asked.

"If she wants to," the older woman answered. Tears gathered in her eyes as she put her arm around her daughter. "When it first happened, I was just grateful she would live. As time passed and we faced the real possibility of extensive scarring, I couldn't help wanting her just to be normal. I know it was selfish, but mothers want normal for their kids."

Must be a universal mom thing, Sky thought, remembering what Dom had said about his own mother. "And now?"

"Thanks to Dr. Rodriguez, instead of a trip to the local blacksmith for chain mail, we're on our way to the mall for short skirts and strapless dresses. I just hope her father is as excited about our expanded choices for her wardrobe."

Sky smiled at the two of them. "I'm sure he will be."

"Why are you here to see the doctor?" Kate asked, openly examining her face. "You're so pretty. What work do you need done?"

"I'm just here on an errand," Sky said. "Have a wonderful time shopping."

"We will," Kate said. "Come on, Mom."

The two of them walked out the door and left Sky feeling weird. Dom was a plastic surgeon. She'd thought that meant froufrou medicine. Now she'd seen for herself that his skill had given a young girl back her life. What an awesome gift.

Sky huffed out a breath, then lifted her hand to knock on the receptionist's window, but it was already open. A pretty brunette sat there. A *very* pretty young brunette, she noted. She also noted a slight twisting in her gut, but refused to speculate on what that was all about. Why waste the energy? In a few weeks this would all be over and she'd go back to Black Arrow where she belonged.

"May I help you?" the receptionist asked.

"I'd like to see Dr. Rodriguez. Just for a moment—"

"Do you have an appointment?"

"No. You see I just need to give—"

"The doctor has finished seeing his morning patients.

If you'd like to make an appointment, I can help you with that."

"You don't understand. I just need a moment of the doctor's time—"

"And I would be more than happy to do that for you. When is a good time for you to see Dr. Rodriguez?"

"Now."

"I'm sorry. As I said, office hours are over until this afternoon. Is there another time that would work for you?"

Hmm, Sky mused. Pretty brunette was a pit bull in disguise.

Before she could decide what to do, the doctor in question walked up behind the receptionist. "Sky."

"Hi," she said, raising her hand and wiggling her fingers in greeting. "Doctor, can you squeeze me in?"

Something hot and intense flashed into his eyes. The look disappeared before Sky could identify it.

"You know this woman, Doctor?" the receptionist asked.

"Yes," he said. "She's—"

"His fiancée." Sky couldn't resist. Payback was a stinker. But she owed him for not telling her up front about the whole bed-sharing thing. So far they'd done everything his way. It was time to show Dr. Deceitful the error of his ways.

Dom rubbed a hand across the back of his neck as he cleared his throat. "Grace, this is my fiancée Sky—"

"Actually, Grace," Sky said, interrupting him, "my real name is Shelby Parker. Dom likes to call me Sky. I'm not sure why." She gave him her most dazzling smile.

"Your eyes remind me of storm clouds," he explained, his voice deep and seductive. "Ready to spit out a hurricane one minute or a gentle renewing rain the next."

Sky stared at him. Who knew Dr. Dom had such a poetic soul? Apparently his receptionist agreed if the wide, melty look in her chocolate-brown eyes was anything to go by.

Grace looked at her then back at him. "I confess I suspected you were involved with someone, but I had no idea you were engaged to be married. The invitation to the party you gave me this morning didn't say anything about—"

"Uh, yes," he said, shifting his feet. "It's a surprise. We wanted to announce it together at the party. Isn't that right, sweetheart?"

Sky heard the slightest note of discomfort in his voice and bit the corner of her lip for a moment to keep from smiling. "That's right. But I'm so happy and excited. I simply couldn't keep it to myself. Maybe by then he'll have time to shop for my engagement ring. I hope you don't mind that I let our little secret slip to Grace, Dom."

"Of course not," he said.

The lack of sincerity in his tone paled in comparison to the hot look in his eyes that promised revenge. What form would it take? In a week they would be sharing a bed. Was he the patient type?

No time like the present to get in her licks. Sky braced her elbows on the counter. "After all, Dom, Grace works for you. She runs interference for you. Keeps out the riffraff trying to get an audience with the great and powerful Oz. She should know what's going on. Right, Grace?"

"R-right," Grace said, squirming uncomfortably in her swivel chair.

Dom moved beside the desk inside the reception area and rested a hip on the corner. He glanced at his employee, then his gaze met Sky's. "Grace screens everyone who comes in the office or calls. She carefully processes each one to decide how much time to schedule for a patient so that the wait is kept to a minimum. No one should be able to read *War And Peace* cover to cover while they're waiting for an appointment with me. It's Grace's responsibility to make sure that doesn't happen."

"From firsthand experience I can tell you she does a fine job." Sky admired him for defending his employee. She dug in her purse and pulled out the reason she'd dropped by in the first place. Holding it out she said, "You forgot your beeper." She looked at Grace. "Normally he's so together. He never forgets anything. He puts his socks in the hamper, rinses toothpaste out of the sink and loads his dirty dishes in the dishwasher." She smiled with satisfaction as she noted the exasperated expression on his handsome face.

"How did I ever get along without you?" He took the beeper from her and when his fingers grazed the palm of her hand, shivers streaked up her arm and settled in her chest. "Thanks, honey."

"You're welcome, sweet cheeks."

He shot her a warning look as he nudged his white lab coat aside and clipped the electronic gizmo to his belt. Underneath that coat she knew his white dress shirt was crisply pressed and had long sleeves. His silk tie with its conservative red-and-blue stripes coordinated with his navy slacks. His shoes were expensive leather but not a dress shoe. They were designed for comfort, to be worn by a man whose work kept him on his feet.

Earlier, Sky had noticed his office attire when she'd

fixed breakfast for him. Only she hadn't understood the comfortable shoes as they'd shared coffee and conversation. Now she knew there was more to his doctor skills than she'd thought. Did it mean something that during breakfast he'd looked at his watch, practically turned pale, and leapt to his feet saying, "This never happens. I'm really late." It wasn't until after he'd gone that she'd noticed his beeper sitting on the counter.

Dom looked at her. "You didn't have to bring it all the way down here. I've got cell and office phones. I carry it as a precaution."

"Something tells me you'd clip a communication satellite to your belt to not miss an emergency call," she said.

"Sounds like you know him really well," Grace chimed in. "He's really dedicated."

"Yeah, I'm finding that out. And I didn't mind delivering your beeper." She shrugged. "I wanted to see where the great and powerful Oz works."

"Very funny. You just—"

"Doctor?" Grace interrupted. "If you don't need me, I'm supposed to meet my boyfriend for lunch—"

"Go, Grace."

Standing, she looked at Sky and said, "It was nice to meet you, Shelby. I'll see you at the party."

Sky nodded. "I'll consider that your RSVP. For two?"

Grace nodded. "I'm going to ask Rob, my boyfriend, when I meet him. But I'm sure he'll go. See you later."

"'Bye." Sky lifted a hand in farewell as the girl walked through the door beside the reception desk. Then she left the medical suite.

Well, well, pretty, brunette, pit bull Grace had a boyfriend. Sky felt relief course through her. What was that all about? She would only be relieved if she'd felt threatened. And she shouldn't feel threatened because she and Dom didn't have a relationship. They had a conspiracy.

Hearing herself called Shelby brought home for the first time that she was actually impersonating someone. Her heart dropped to her stomach, then seemed to bounce up and lodge in her throat.

"You okay? You look like something didn't agree with you." Dom straightened away from the desk.

"Good call, Doc." Lying didn't sit well with her and she'd just gotten a glimpse of what the next few weeks were going to be like. But the invitations had gone out. Splitting for home and leaving him in the lurch didn't sit well with her, either. Somehow pretending to be his fiancée felt like the lesser of two evils.

She smiled brightly at him. "How long has Grace worked for you?"

"About two years, I guess. Why?"

"Just wondering why she's afraid of you." Sky shrugged as she stuck her hands into the pockets of her jeans.

He looked surprised. "That's ridiculous. Where did you get an idea like that?"

"The way she looked at you, I guess. Trying to read you, make sure she hadn't messed up." Sky recognized the look after years of wearing it herself.

"She's a very efficient receptionist and I'm sure she's not scared of me after all this time."

"Of course. What was I thinking?"

"Want to see the rest of the office?" he asked.

"Sure."

She followed him as he pointed with pride to the tidy, sterile yet comfortable exam rooms, the outpatient surgery area, and his own office, complete with desk and computer. Sky rested a hip against the leather wing chair in the room.

"I thought you were a plastic surgeon," she said.

"You thought right."

"I mean, I thought plastic surgery was breast augmentation and designer noses."

"It can be. But there's a lot more to it than that."

"So I found out." At his puzzled look she said, "I ran into Kate and her mom on their way out. She said you treated her burns."

He nodded. "That's my specialty. Once the life-threatening trauma is past, a burn victim wants to get on with life. They don't want to stand out, to be different."

"And they can't if they're scarred?"

"That's right. Technology and procedures are constantly changing. I use the latest techniques to minimize scarring. In the most severe cases, even I can't help."

For just an instant Sky caught a glimpse of intense frustration in his eyes. "And you can't stand that. When there's nothing you can do."

"I use my powers for good, remember? If I can't do good, then—" He hesitated, looking at a spot over her head. "Yeah, I hate it a lot."

"Well, I have to apologize."

"For what?" he asked, surprised. "Did you put a dent in my Beemer?"

She smiled as she shook her head. Somehow she knew something as insignificant as a dented fender wouldn't phase him. But a scarred teenage girl who couldn't wear short skirts and shoulder-baring party dresses would keep him awake nights.

"I thought you were a designer doc. There's a lot more to plastic surgery than I knew. I'm sorry I underestimated you."

"Don't mention it." He took off his white coat and hung it on the back of his office chair. "Can I take you to lunch? It's the least I can do to thank you for delivering my beeper."

"I've got other plans. I wish I could."

Which was why she couldn't. She was starting to wish for things that would never happen. The trick was to harden her heart—the consistency of a diamond would be good.

Chapter Six

Dom drove the SUV up his street and noted that his house was lit up like a church on Christmas. A strange, unfamiliar feeling of contentment slipped over him. He'd driven this street every day for the past five years, but he couldn't remember such a heightened state of awareness before.

He knew his anticipation had less to do with the welcoming lights than the welcoming woman he knew was inside. This was a sensation he'd never experienced before, this intense pleasure and satisfaction just because he was home. At least he hadn't felt it before Sky had been there.

Shelby was the only woman he'd shared his home with—until Sky. His former fiancée had lived with him longer yet he'd never felt the way he did now, as if he couldn't wait to see her. What was going on with him? His bride-to-be hadn't been gone that long and—

He snapped his fingers. That explained everything. First she was there, then she was gone and no one had waited for him. He'd found it pleasant to come home to a woman. His intense reaction to Sky's presence was merely the contrast of coming home to no one. Although that didn't explain why his body hummed with anticipation and his heart raced as if he'd run a marathon. That had never happened with Shelby. But it had the first night he'd come home to Sky. The feeling had only intensified since then.

But maybe it was about her turning down his lunch proposal when she'd dropped off his beeper. The depth of his disappointment that day had surprised him, considering he hadn't expected to see her at all. For God's sake. Since when did he second guess this touchy-feely stuff? There were more important ways to use his energy.

He got out of the car and slammed the door, then walked into the house, going through the laundry room to the kitchen. Instantly, mouth-watering aromas surrounded him—along with something he couldn't hear, see, touch, taste or smell. It was a warmth and peace that went soul-deep. Sky walked in from the dining room and he knew she was that something and he could hear, see, touch, taste and smell her.

As soon as she saw him, an instantaneous welcoming smile curved the corners of her lush mouth. "Hi."

"Hi, yourself," he said. He set his briefcase beside the island. "Something smells good."

"Chicken and dumplings."

"Sounds good." He looked at the barren table in the eating area. "Want me to get out the plates and set the table?"

She shook her head, eyes bright with some secret. "Already done."

"I'm going to take a wild guess and say it's done in the dining room."

"Correct, Doctor. You win an all-expense paid trip into said dining room for the works."

"Uh-oh."

"Fear not, intrepid physician. The works includes flowers and candles, fine linen tablecloth with matching napkins, the good china and crystal. Remind me to ask how come you have all that stuff."

"Mom."

"'Nuff said. I've also got a lovely bottle of chardonnay chilling in the fridge. Now that you're here, let the works begin."

She stood in the center of the kitchen, about two feet from him. Apparently she was dressed for "the works" casual. In hot-pink fleece pants and matching top, with thick white socks on her feet, she was casual sexy. Her shiny black hair was pulled on top of her head with a cloth scrunchy thing and wisps caressed the back of her neck. Her cheeks were pink; he couldn't decide whether or not it was from the cooking or the reflection of her sweatshirt. Whatever, she looked more mouth-watering than her cooking smelled. There was nothing casual about the way she made him feel.

He wanted to pull her into his arms and kiss her until they were on fire and set off the smoke detector.

He took a deep breath instead. "I can hardly wait. Do I have time to change?" Translation: could he go to his corner and compose himself before he lost his head and did something he would regret?

"Sure. You slip into something more comfortable and I'll pour you a glass of wine."

With every chromosome of his being he wished he'd said those words to her. If he had, there would have been a very different subtext. But she meant them completely literally because she was just play-acting. He was having a great deal of trouble remembering that.

"I'll be back in a flash."

"No flashing, please," she said, her cheeks turning pinker if possible.

"I wouldn't think of it." A bald-faced lie. He'd been thinking of hardly anything else *but* both of them naked.

He left her long enough to change out of his slacks, dress shirt, tie and sport coat into faded jeans and flannel shirt. Then he hurried back to the kitchen.

"Dinner is served," she said.

"I'm starved." That was a perfectly normal, completely innocent response until his gaze strayed involuntarily to her mouth. He'd tasted that particular feast once before and discovered she was a sensual smorgasbord.

For the second time in as many minutes he was in an acute state of arousal. He felt retreat was the better part of discretion and quickly sat behind one of the place settings at the dining room table. Steam rose from the contents of the plate Sky had placed there. As hot as he felt, it wouldn't surprise him to find steam coming out of his ears. This was ridiculous. He was behaving like a teenage boy who'd just experienced for the first time the potent chemical reaction of testosterone.

He'd made it through high school. He'd conquered college, medical school, internship and double residency. Surely he could master this inexplicable, involuntary, inconvenient, inappropriate attraction to Sky Colton.

"So," he said, turning his attention away from things he couldn't control to the formal table she'd set. "Care to explain the royal treatment?"

It was obvious she'd gone to a great deal of trouble. The question was, why?

"I felt like it." Sitting at a right angle to him, Sky took a sip of her wine.

"O-o-kay." He cut a piece of the chicken breast and tasted it. The pleasant flavors of wine and herbs were released in his mouth. "Wow, this is great."

"I sense we have a trust issue."

"Then you need to have a sensory checkup. I'm telling the truth. This is delicious."

"That's not what I meant. There were all kinds of subtle undercurrents in that 'okay.' You don't believe I felt like fussing with dinner?"

"Of course I believe. Or you wouldn't have. However I feel obligated to point out, if only in my own defense, that this is the fifth time you've cooked dinner in my home."

"Give the doctor a gold-plated stethoscope. He can count." She finished the wine in her glass.

His body vibrated, sending him into a pleasurable state of expectation. When she went into debate mode, he was completely taken with her.

"On four of those occasions," he continued, ignoring her sarcasm, "my dinner was served on a plastic-covered plate warmed in the microwave. While I appreciate the fact that you kept me company in the kitchen as I consumed my food, you had already eaten."

"A person could collapse from starvation waiting for you. You should know how dangerous low blood sugar can be."

"So why did you wait for me tonight?"

"I don't know. It's Friday."

"Date night?" he asked, unable to resist baiting her.

"Date? You and I?" She laughed. "We skipped that

portion of the mating ritual and went straight to cohabitation."

"Mating ritual," he commented. "Is that what this is called?"

"Normally it would be." She picked up her glass then put it down because it was empty. "But this is special circumstances. We're pretending to be engaged and thereby engaged in an act of deception or misrepresentation."

"Have you been reading the dictionary?"

"I looked up the word *fraud.* It was my greatest hope that I'd exaggerated and was being overly dramatic in my characterization of what we're doing as illegal."

"No such luck?"

"We are bad to the bone."

"Still, to characterize it as criminal, I think there has to be the intention of causing harm. We're doing quite the opposite."

"Are we? I'm not so sure," she said, shaking her head.

"You have a knack for taking a conversation on a tangent in order to keep from answering the tough questions."

"Like why the royal treatment?"

"Exactly."

"Well, Doctor, you're going to force me into a confession."

"This should be good." He picked up the half-empty bottle of wine and refilled her glass. "You might need this."

"Thanks." She lifted the delicate crystal to her lips and sipped. "I guess it's my way of saying I'm sorry for misjudging you."

"We've already been through this." That day in his

office when she turned him down for lunch. ''I don't hold a grudge.''

''Maybe I do. At myself. I thought you were all about shallowness, beauty is only skin deep, appearance is everything. Cosmetic sort of doctoring.''

He took a bite of chicken and chewed thoughtfully. ''I'll admit I chose to specialize in plastic surgery with dollar signs in my eyes. I grew up poor.'' Enough said, he thought. ''Cosmetic surgery can be lucrative. Today's culture panders to the beauty myth and a lot of people are willing to spend their disposable income in the pursuit of physical perfection. But that's not all it's about. There are all kinds of reconstructive cases—the child with a cleft palate, dog bites, a car accident where the passenger goes through the windshield.''

''I never thought about it,'' she said.

''Good. That means life-changing trauma hasn't touched you.''

He didn't want to think about anything bad ever happening to her. A feeling of protectiveness for her swelled in his chest. When his scheme was over and his mother safely on her cruise, Sky would go back home. The idea of not seeing her, not knowing if she was okay, bothered him. But that made absolutely no sense.

''Did you always specialize in burns?''

Thinking back, he met her gaze. ''I saw a little girl in the E.R., four or five years old. Firemen pulled her out of her burning home—electrical fire, I think. She had burns over seventy-five percent of her body.'' He ran his fingers through his hair. ''God, she was a fighter. Never complained. I wanted so badly to help her.''

''What happened?'' She rested her palm on his hand.

He found the warmth of her fingers, the connection to another person, oddly comforting. He turned his hand,

intertwining his fingers with hers as their gazes met. ''She died. Infection set in and her heart just gave out.'' He let out a long breath as he recalled his frustration, profound disappointment—rage. ''I never ever want to feel that helpless again, so I go to seminars, study new techniques, read medical journals, gather all the new information I can.''

She squeezed his palm reassuringly. ''You can't save everyone.''

''Yeah. But knowing that doesn't help a whole lot when you lose a child. So I try never to let that happen.''

''Do you see many children in your practice?''

''Some. Once a week I spend time at a county clinic in downtown Houston to do what I can. International relief organizations bring kids here from Third World countries for medical treatment.'' He thought about the damage he'd seen to some of those little faces and shook his head against the memories. ''I do what I can to reconstruct their features and make them look normal. Some people call it a miracle. The miracle would be to have no trauma in the world.''

''I had no idea.'' Sympathy swam in her gray eyes as she left her hand in his. ''Obviously your practice is more than burn patients.''

He nodded, oddly grateful for the contact and wishing it never had to end. ''Fortunately we don't see one of those every five minutes. But when I'm needed, the practice comes to a halt and I stay with the patient for the day, or until he's stabilized. The teen with a bump on her nose is rescheduled. It's not an emergency, but she'll get seen because her feelings of self-esteem and self-worth are important.''

She nodded. ''I found that out when I met Kate and her mother.''

"Yeah. For children—teenagers—plastic surgery makes a profound difference. Instead of withdrawing during the remainder of her high school years, Kate will blossom. At her age, social stuff spills over into the academic and it all blends together to build character. She'll have the confidence to try anything, be anything."

Looking as if she felt guilty, Sky shook her head. "I so underestimated you and what you do—what you're all about. I'm so sorry. I have to apologize again."

"Accepted. Can we let it go now?" He hadn't talked about that to anyone. Not even his mother. And he really wanted to change the subject.

"I guess I'm having trouble doing that because I've experienced that very thing."

"How?" Anyone even casually acquainted with this beautiful, exciting woman couldn't possibly underestimate her. Not if they had half a brain. "I guess the more pertinent question is, who?"

She sighed. "My family. Some of it is overprotectiveness. But a lot of it is…they just don't get me."

"Isn't that the lament of most teenagers?" She hardly looked older than one. Her fresh youthfulness made him feel like a dirty old man. Another good reason, as if he needed one, to purge this strange attraction for her from his system.

"Is it? Even if I could, I wouldn't be a teen again for anything. The difference is, now I don't care if anyone understands me. Ah, the perks of growing old."

"You don't know what old is. I could give lessons."

"You're not old. To me. Although Kate said you were pretty cute for an old guy."

"Thanks. I feel much better now," he said ruefully.

She laughed, but her smile dimmed quickly and turned a little sad around the edges. "You probably noticed that my father and brothers and a cousin or two are somehow involved in upholding the law. My mother is a retired teacher. Considering that, how do you suppose they all felt when I started designing jewelry?"

He shrugged as he tried to put himself in her family's shoes. "I guess they were less than thrilled."

"Bingo. But by then I'd given myself permission to be who I am and let go of any suspicion that my mother had slept with the mailman."

"Yeah, because all the best jewelry designers got their DNA from U.S. postal service employees."

She grinned. "You're approaching it from a scientific perspective, the whole gene thing. I saw it as an emotional issue."

"Which was?"

"I didn't fit in. And, actually, it's not past tense. I don't fit in now." She pulled her hand from his grasp.

He wanted to tell her the diagnosis wouldn't fly. She fit like a glove in his life. His acute feelings of expectation when he'd arrived home were proof. And if he said any of that to her, she would call him crazy.

"Yeah, I saw the way you didn't fit in. I watched you in the courthouse with the guys."

"You've never been to a family get-together where we talk about what everyone else is doing. Oh, there's always a cursory question about how my business is going. Then it's back to the ups and downs of catching perps. It's all about the good of the many outweighing the feelings of the one."

"They love you, Sky. I saw it for myself."

"I know. And I love them. Which is why I keep trying. Distributing the mug shot of Kenny Randolph was me attempting to conform to family traditions."

"Give me another example of you not fitting in. I bet you can't."

"I wish. This one's easy. I couldn't adapt to my fiancé's expectations."

Dom was so stunned he didn't know how to respond. She'd been engaged? It had never once crossed his mind to wonder about her love life or why she wasn't married. He didn't want to believe he'd been that self-absorbed and chalked it up to the fact he'd been too grateful she was available.

"And what were his expectations?" Dom finally asked.

"He's an accountant. Started his own firm. He said one business in a family is enough. He expected me to have babies and stay home to raise them."

"And you didn't want to give up jewelry design?"

"I'm flexible. We could have compromised that one to a mutually agreeable solution."

"What was the deal-breaker?"

"When he told me not to reveal to his parents that I'm part Comanche Indian. He was concerned about the fact getting out and how it would look."

Everything Dom wanted to say involved a four-letter word not fit for a lady's ears. But that explained something he'd been wondering about. The night he'd brought her here, she'd said the place was big enough and he wouldn't get under her skin. She'd tried to pretend she'd meant something else, but he hadn't bought the act. She'd been hurt once upon a time and wanted to put a safe zone around herself—not let anyone close enough to do it again. If anyone understood, it was him.

He let out a long breath. "What did you do?"

"I broke it off." She looked at him, shadows wavering in her eyes, her mouth tight with pain. "Looking back, I realize he was a jerk. But it took me a long time. And until I did, it hurt a lot. But the message I got was that because of who and what I am, I wouldn't fit in his world."

"You're right about one thing."

"What's that?" she asked, frowning.

"He's a jerk. Want me to hunt him down and beat him up for you?"

She laughed. "Thanks for the offer. But I wouldn't want you to damage your hands. They're pretty valuable."

"So are yours—the hands of an artist."

"But you save lives. I create jewelry. Not even in the same league."

"Do professions have to be equal? Doesn't the work each individual chooses to do have value? If everyone on earth was a doctor—"

"What?"

"For one thing, we'd all starve."

She laughed. "Good point. Not to mention doctors keep inhuman hours."

"No argument there. Any woman who throws her lot in with a doctor needs to have her head examined."

"Why?" she asked, resting her cheek in her palm as she absently pushed food around her plate with her fork.

"She needs to understand what she's getting into. Do you know how high the divorce rate is among doctors?"

"Not a clue."

"Me, either. But I'll bet it's higher than the average because it's such a demanding job. There's not much time left for a personal life after office hours, hospital rounds, calls at all hours of the night to deal with a crisis, plans canceled unexpectedly when you're called to the

E.R. for a burn victim on the way in. Sometimes I meet the patient in the field. It's not easy on a relationship."

"No kidding."

"That's why the woman involved must have a life of her own. She needs to make friends easily so she'll have a support group. It also helps so she can mingle with her significant other's colleagues, but maintain her independence so she doesn't need him. That way he's free to do his work."

"Those are pretty hefty qualifications. No wonder you waited so long to take the plunge."

"Shelby met all of those requirements and my mother was impressed by her background. She would have made me a perfect wife."

"I'm sorry it didn't work out, Dom." Sympathy pooled in her eyes.

He waited for the pain to hit him. Oddly, it never came. He didn't need her consolation. Dom looked at Sky, so lovely and fragile. So sweet and funny and feisty and— Whoa!

This lovely, vibrant, intelligent, stubborn woman drove every other thought from his mind. And it seemed she was making a habit of it. But this time the idea that stopped him cold wasn't about her. It was just plain unbelievable.

He didn't miss Shelby.

Dom suddenly realized that his only thoughts about her had been afterthoughts. Or comparisons to explain his instant and powerful attraction to Sky. But he had to face the truth: he didn't miss Shelby at all, not since he'd first seen Sky Colton. What was he supposed to do with that information?

Obviously he didn't know the first thing about love.

More important, what was it about Sky that evoked

such a potent, consuming response from him? If he had the answer to that question, he would also have a solution.

And he needed one—*bad.* Because he didn't want to make a fool of himself again. Unfortunately, that was a clear and present danger since his family would arrive soon, forcing him to share his bedroom with Sky.

In close, intimate quarters, how was he supposed to control his attraction, fascination—temptation?

Chapter Seven

Sky felt as if she were going to throw up. Today was D day—Operation Deception. Lying through her teeth would commence any minute.

Dom was picking up his mother and grandmother from the airport while Sky moved the last of her things from the upstairs guest quarters into the master bedroom. His walk-in closet was half-empty, which made her sad for some reason. Maybe guilt was tap dancing on her soul again. If not for her big mouth, Shelby's clothes would be hanging beside his.

But she had dispensed advice and, sage though it was, she'd cost him the perfect wife. Now Sky was doing everything she could to make up for it. Including sharing his room for a week.

Next to his suits and sport coats, she placed her things—several sweaters, skirts, a couple of pairs of slacks, and a dress or two. Shaking her head, she realized the pitiful assortment didn't make it look as though she actually lived there.

Glancing into the dressing area, she surveyed her toiletries by one sink and his by the other. She'd arranged their things the way she imagined a committed couple would have them. Once upon a time, she'd thought she was half of a committed couple. Then she'd found out it was impossible to be intensely involved with a man who was ashamed of you. She knew better than to make that mistake again. Especially with a man who approached marriage as if it were a business merger.

So why did the thought of Dom turn her insides to liquid and her knees to meringue? Temporary insanity, she thought, leaving the dressing area. She'd get over it.

Or not, she thought, looking at the bed. It was quite an attractive one, and certainly large enough for two people to share. Without any part of their bodies touching. That teeny, tiny thought evoked a profound yearning deep inside her that was almost a palpable pain.

She wanted Dominic Rodriguez.

Until that night in her apartment when he'd held her and kissed her, it had been a long time since she'd experienced physical closeness with a man. She'd absorbed it as fast as dry beach sand soaked up the rising tide. And she craved more of the same. That's what this temptation was all about. Identifying the problem was the first step in solving it.

Who was she kidding? This was never going to work. Pretend lovers by day, virtual strangers sharing a bed by night. What had she been thinking to agree to this? Guilt was a powerful weapon. Especially when a man as sexy as Dominic Rodriguez wielded it.

She'd been in his home for two weeks now. She was as comfortable in his environment as it was possible to be when she was so attracted to a man seriously on the rebound. But she'd been able to keep it under control—

while they were in separate rooms on different floors of his house. What would happen while they shared a bed?

There was no way to avoid finding out. Unless she was prepared to spoil his carefully constructed plan to keep from disappointing his mother. Sky knew she had to make this work. Somehow.

That meant she had to act like a woman in love when she met his family. This wasn't going to be easy.

She heard a car in the drive, then the sound of slamming doors. The nerves in her stomach kicked up like a majorette in a marching band.

"It's show time. Break a leg," she said to herself.

Trying to control her nerves, she walked through the family room to the foyer and opened the front door. Two women were making their way along the sidewalk. The first was white-haired and fragile-looking. The younger one was slim and fit and had dark hair sprinkled with silver. Both were small, shorter than her own five feet six. Behind them, Dom followed, carrying suitcases. "Mama, *Abuelita,* this is my bride-to-be."

"Hello." Sky moved onto the brick porch and waited for further introductions. She hadn't told Dom that she planned to use her given name. That way, she was less likely to trip up. When the two women were beside her she said, "It's a pleasure to meet you. Please call me Sky. Dom does. It's his pet name for me."

Dom stopped behind the older woman and lifted one eyebrow quizzically as he met Sky's gaze. "Sky, this is Isabel Castillo, my *abuelita*—grandmother."

"How do you do?" she said, holding out her hand.

"You can call me Mrs. Castillo." Her cultured voice was like steel and her English perfect, even though the words were laced with an accent. The blue-eyed woman regarded her with cautious interest before taking her outstretched hand. "Why does he call you Sky?"

"It's nothing." Dom put the suitcases down in the foyer and draped his arm across the other woman's shoulders. "And this is Victoria Rodriguez, my mother."

"Dom has told me so much about you," Sky said, holding out her hand again. "I'm so pleased to finally meet you."

"And I you. Dominic's fiancée. Please call me Victoria. I can hardly wait until you can officially call me Mama." Her Spanish accent was very subtle yet made her tone friendly and inviting. The woman pulled her into a firm embrace. Then she stepped back, still gripping Sky's upper arms. "But why does my son call you Sky?"

"He says my eyes remind him of storm clouds, ready to spit out a hurricane one minute or a gentle renewing rain the next." She shrugged as she met his curious gaze, then looked at his mother. "Who knew that serious, intimidating exterior hid the heart and soul of a poet?"

"I'm not intimidating," he argued.

"Some people call him StoneHeart," Sky offered.

"He doesn't smile enough. But now that he has you, it will change." Victoria glanced fondly up at him. "He's a man of many surprises, my son."

"Yes, he is," Sky answered sincerely.

That day in his office, the explanation about her eyes to his shocked receptionist had amazed her at the same time it tugged at her heart. Which was why she recalled it so vividly. She wondered if he wondered about her remembering what he'd said, word for word. His expression gave nothing away.

"Please come inside." She moved back for them to pass in front of her. "Welcome."

Dom waited until they were in the house before moving beside her. He pulled her into his arms and kissed her, intimately. Lifting his head, he said, "I missed you, sweetheart."

In spite of the liquid heat coursing through her, Sky knew his warning expression meant not to call him sweet cheeks. "It seemed an eternity that you were gone, my love."

Uh-oh. That came out way too easy. She stepped out of his embrace, but he nestled her to his side with one arm around her waist. She followed his lead and they stood there joined at the hip with her so hot an egg would fry on her forehead. Glancing shyly at his relatives she said, "I hope you're hungry."

"Airplane food." Mrs. Castillo shook her head, a disapproving look on her lined face.

"Good. I made a quiche from scratch and salad and fruit."

"That sounds wonderful," Victoria said.

"I thought you do not cook," the older woman commented.

Sky's heart hammered. What did his grandmother know about Shelby? She sensed a minefield ahead and met Dom's gaze, looking for guidance. A subtle lift of his shoulders told her she would get no help from Mr. Don't-Worry-It-Will-Be-Easy.

Why had she thrown in details? She could have just said it was frozen. Had she been trying to impress them? So they would like her? If she was actually marrying the man, it would make sense. Since she wasn't, there was no explanation other than she was becoming a very good liar. Come to think of it, she'd rather be a good liar than try to make them like her because she had expectations of a relationship with him. Not happening.

Frantically she searched for an explanation to smooth over the slip. ''I haven't cooked much, but a wife takes care of her husband so I figured I should learn. I've been practicing.''

''Hmm,'' was all the older woman said.

''Let me take your coats.'' Sky moved away from Dom and held out her hands.

After she'd hung up the two jackets, she led the way into the kitchen. ''Would you care for something to drink? Iced tea? Hot tea? Coffee?''

''Hot tea,'' they both said together.

''Let me get it,'' Victoria said, moving to the cupboard. ''I'm not a guest. I've been here many times. In fact I helped him decorate. Besides I'm used to taking care of others.''

''Well, I—''

Dom cleared his throat. ''Sky's used to taking care of herself. Aren't you?''

''Yes,'' she agreed.

''Really?'' Victoria put a teakettle filled with water on a burner to heat. ''I should think you would be accustomed to being waited on. Dom said your father made a lot of money in the oil business. Surely he has an estate with a large staff.''

''He does,'' Sky answered lamely. Probably. How would she know? More important—how did she get herself into this hellish situation? Oh, yes. Dom. She shot him a glare.

''You must let me fuss over you,'' Victoria insisted, bustling around the kitchen to make tea.

''But I'm happier when I keep busy.''

''Busy?'' Mrs. Castillo said, subtle disapproval in the

single word. She stood ramrod straight on the other side of the work island. "Doing what?"

Sky wondered about her barely concealed hostility. It seemed as if the older woman didn't like her. Correction—she didn't like Shelby. Rather than make up a lie about how she occupied her time, she decided to weave in some truth that she could remember. "I design jewelry."

"Is that so? I thought my grandson would fall in love with someone who shared his profession. A doctor or nurse perhaps."

Dom moved next to the older woman and draped his arm across her shoulders. "*Abuelita,* you should see the set of rings Sky designed for our wedding. The bands are etched with our initials and they're exquisite." Briefly he met her gaze and his own sparkled with humor. He'd stolen her weave-some-truth-into-the-lie technique. "You should not judge someone until you get to know them."

"It's all right," Sky said. "My father feels the same way about what I do."

Victoria looked at her mother. "Dom is right about not judging, Mama. If designing jewelry makes Sky happy, no one should question it." She tapped her lip. "That reminds me. I want to see the engagement ring my son gave you." She grabbed Sky's hand and stared at her bare ring finger. Then she looked questioningly at her son. "Dominic?"

"He doesn't have time to shop. He's a very busy doctor," Sky said, jumping in to defend him. Why did she feel compelled to save his bacon? She'd pointed out the very same thing to him. Maybe because he'd come to her defense just moments ago. "I don't need an engagement ring."

''Sensible,'' his grandmother said grudgingly.

''Of course you should have a ring,'' Victoria protested. ''I so wanted him to have a traditional courtship, engagement and wedding. I know you're a busy doctor and you're very important to your patients. But you need a life, too.''

''I have one. Now that Sky is here. Wedding stuff won't change the fact that she's filled a place in my life that was empty until I met her.''

As he talked, Sky watched the expression on his face. Complete sincerity. She knew everything was make-believe, yet *she* believed him. For a heartbeat, she wished they weren't pretending. She wished they were in love for real.

The teakettle whistled and Victoria poured hot water into the two cups she'd set on the counter. ''Speaking of traditional, let me see your wedding announcement in the newspaper.''

Dom cleared his throat. ''We haven't done that, Mama. We're trying to keep this quiet. Sky is a wealthy woman and the tabloids would stalk her for a story.''

''But it's customary. We'll have a photograph taken tomorrow and put in the newspaper. No one will notice, but we can put the clipping in your wedding album.''

''That sounds lovely,'' Sky said lamely.

''I'm glad you approve, dear. Now, tell me about your wedding dress. I would ask to see it, but I'm sure it's not here. You no doubt left it at the bridal shop since my son is impetuous and impatient. With him around, there would be no surprise when you walk down the aisle.''

Sky could have kissed the woman for giving her an out. She could describe anything. ''I've always wanted a very full skirt so that my waist will look small. Satin,

I think. And strapless.'' She glanced at Dom and caught a look of such breathtaking intensity in his eyes it made her heart skip. The expression told her he was visualizing the dress. And liked what he saw.

''Strapless?'' Mrs. Castillo chimed in. ''That would show off your new breasts.''

''Excuse me?'' Sky said. If she'd been drinking anything, it would have backed up and come out her nose.

''Yes. It's how you met my grandson. He did…how do you say it? Breast—'' She held her hands away from her own chest to show what she meant.

''Augmentation?'' he supplied.

''That's it. A strapless dress would be the best way to advertise what a good doctor he is.'' The older woman looked her over, focusing on her chest. ''I thought you would be bigger—Anna Nicole Smith or Pamela Anderson bigger.''

The mystery procedure he'd done on Shelby was a secret no longer. But how in the world did his grandmother know? She looked at Dom for an explanation.

Again he lifted his shoulders slightly as if to say he hadn't a clue. ''Sky is perfect just the way she is.''

''I agree. My son is a good doctor.''

''*My* grandson is the finest physician,'' Mrs. Castillo added.

''Let's change the subject,'' he said. ''It's getting deep in here.''

''We were discussing your dress.'' Victoria clapped her palms together. ''It sounds lovely. When are you going to take us to the shop to see it?''

Minefield. Since the moment the two women had walked in, everything she'd said exploded in her face. She didn't have a wedding dress. How was she going to recover from this blast?

Her mind raced. Normally truth worked best, although her success rate today wouldn't hold up to the theory. But she would keep trying, after she came up with a plausible prevarication.

"You want to see it? I'm sorry. I thought you said what kind of dress did I *want.* I haven't actually bought a wedding gown yet."

"But, Sky," Victoria protested. "The ceremony is right after Mama and I return from the cruise. You haven't much time."

"I know what I want. It won't take long to find something," she said weakly.

Victoria snapped her fingers. "I have an idea. We'll shop this week. Since you're going to be the daughter I didn't give birth to, you must let me help. It would give me a great deal of pleasure."

She met Dom's gaze and he nodded slightly. If she couldn't distract his mother from this mission, she had to remember to get his credit card.

"Okay," she said. "That would be fun."

Sky decided it was way past time she changed the subject to something completely innocent. What could be more innocuous than house decor?

She looked at Dom's mother. "I love the way you decorated the house, Victoria. I especially like the antique credenza in the foyer and the four-poster bed in his—I mean, our room. The two pieces are in beautiful shape and completely lovely and romantic."

"I thought you wanted to redecorate," Mrs. Castillo interjected. "You told me you wanted to get rid of the old furniture and replace it with modern pieces. I believe you said glass, chrome and black lacquer are more your style."

A puzzled expression crossed Dom's face as he

looked down at the older woman. ''How do you know all this, *Abuelita?* You've never met Sky before. Are you psychic?''

She made a sound that was part snort, part laugh. ''Not unless that fancy computer you gave me made me that way. Shelby—I mean, Sky—and I have been talking through e-mail. But you have not written recently. Why?''

''I guess I've been busy,'' Sky answered. What else could she say?

The older woman stared hard at her. ''I have to say you're not what I expected, which goes to show, you can't judge someone until you meet them.''

Sky looked at Dom who shrugged yet again. She could hardly wait to tell him what was on her mind. Later he would get an earful. Unfortunately that conversation would be in his bedroom and they would be alone.

Dom turned down the comforter, then stretched out on the far side of the bed. With acute anticipation, he waited for Sky to come out of the bathroom. In spite of the fact she'd been shooting daggers at him since learning his grandmother had been electronically communicating with Shelby. He knew Sky would have a thing or three hundred to say on the subject and for reasons that eluded him, he couldn't wait. Finally the light in the dressing area went out and she walked into the room.

She was wearing pajamas that looked more like long johns. One piece. Pink. The soft fabric molded to her slender body, revealing every womanly curve. Very feminine. More skin was hidden than exposed, yet she was the most arousing sight he'd seen in longer than he cared to remember. If only the heat in her gaze was sexual passion instead of the kind that drove a woman to slap her man silly.

She put her hands on her gently rounded hips. "Today could have gone worse, but I'm not sure how. How many times did I blow it. Three? Four? Forty?" She let out a long breath. "You've withheld several vital pieces of information from me. Is it because you thought I wouldn't have agreed to this insane idea?"

"Would you?"

"I don't know."

"Do you want to back out?" he asked. Say no, he thought, before he could suppress it.

She shook her head. "And you want to know why? Because now that I've met them, I like your relatives. Your mother wants a daughter. She wants to be included in wedding gown shopping. How sweet is that?"

"And my grandmother?"

"A little blunt. Doesn't hold anything back. Doesn't trust me, which makes her pretty smart."

"She thinks you're Shelby."

Sky folded her arms over her breasts. "I don't know what's up with that. But, she's a hoot. I can't back out now. It would break their hearts. Now that I've met them, how can I do that?"

"Why did you agree in the first place, Sky?"

She moved farther into the room and sat on the end of the bed, as far away from him as she could get. "Redemption. And guilt, I guess. And not all of it is about you or what I said to Shelby about following her heart. I still stand by that, in case you were wondering."

"I wasn't. But what other guilt and redemption could you possibly have?"

"I told you I was engaged once."

He nodded. "The jerk."

"Right. And I broke it off. What I didn't tell you is that I did it at the rehearsal dinner the night before the wedding. It wasn't at the altar, but practically. His parents flew in for the ceremony. I hadn't met them yet and he asked me not to reveal that I'm one-quarter Comanche on my father's side."

"I'm asking you not to reveal something, too."

"It's different. For you, I'm pretending to be someone else. He couldn't accept who I am."

"Under the circumstances you had no choice but to end it."

"My timing was lousy."

"No. His character was lousy *and* his timing. He picked a bad moment to reveal his true feelings. How could you go through with the wedding after that?"

"I know. But money had been spent. He was embarrassed in front of his family and friends. I couldn't do anything about that. Maybe, subconsciously, I figured by helping you I could achieve some cosmic redemption."

"You owe that guy nothing."

"Or maybe this penance would help me learn to keep my mouth shut and not dispense unsolicited advice."

"Okay." But he didn't believe that any more than he thought his wedding-that-never-was situation was anything like Sky's.

"Okay." She sighed as she shifted her position on the bed. "But we have more important things to discuss. Like assessing battle damage. What are we going to do?"

What any mutually attracted man and woman normally did in bed, he thought. He looked at her, sitting primly across from him. Yearning slammed him in the chest with the force of a locomotive. Desire sluiced through him, heating his blood.

"What are we going to do about what?" His voice was rough, raspy.

"Come on, Dom. You were there. I tripped up so many times it was starting to look like pratfall central. If your relatives don't think I'm a fraud, at the very least they believe Shelby's been taken over by aliens. Why didn't you tell me your grandmother has been e-mailing with Shelby?"

"Because I didn't know."

"At the risk of opening a healing wound, what you and Shelby had was a failure to communicate."

"Thanks for the diagnosis."

"Things are just jim-dandy." She slid off the bed and started to pace. "Now your grandmother thinks my breasts are fake and it's all your fault."

"I performed the procedure."

"That's not what I meant. It's your fault for not knowing that she knew. If I'd known she knew, I could have put socks or tissues in my—" She stopped. "Never mind. The point is, I looked ridiculous. Your grandmother no doubt thinks I'm a shallow slacker who's not good enough for you."

"No. She thinks Shelby Parker is not for me. She doesn't know anything about you."

"Yeah, she does. She thinks I dabble in jewelry. My decorating taste is inspired by bad science fiction, and I'm an idiot who can't cook."

He unfolded his arms from his bare chest and noticed her swallow deeply at the movement. Was she as aware of him as he was of her? He slid to the end of the bed and saw her eyes widen. "She admitted the quiche was good."

"How could she deny it after a hefty second helping?

But you're missing the point. How could you not know Shelby was baring her soul to your grandmother?''

Good question. Something else to puzzle through on top of the fact that he didn't miss her. Maybe he was the kind of man who went from one woman to the next because he wouldn't know love if it came in for an office visit. He'd spent time with his bride-to-be. He'd asked her to marry him. She dumped him and now he didn't miss her—thanks to Sky. What he knew about relationships would fit on the head of a pin.

''I have no excuse, Sky. All I can tell you is most of what my grandmother said was news to me.''

''So you were aware that Shelby hated the way this house is decorated and wanted to defile everything you've done with glass, chrome and black lacquer?''

''Yes.'' Now he knew Sky liked the decor, a fact that pleased him very much. Although in the scheme of things her approval was pretty meaningless. In a week this charade would be over and she would be gone. Things would go back to normal—and that thought bothered the hell out of him.

''You could have told me,'' she said.

''Sorry. It slipped my mind.''

She shot him an exasperated look. ''You're so cool, calm and collected. Doesn't anything rattle that annoying serenity of yours?''

''I'm a doctor. Trained for emergencies. Nothing gets to me.''

Except you, he thought. The idea of her leaving rattled him a lot. Only the sight of her in pink long johns and white socks bothered him more. She tied him in knots and cranked his heart rate up without trying. Her porcelain skin was scrubbed free of makeup and her dark hair was pulled to the top of her head, held there by some poufy, rubber-bandy thing. The look was artless and adorable.

Serene? Not hardly. He wanted to pull her into his arms and kiss her until they set off the smoke detectors again. But that was the worst thing he could do. Because he already knew more about her than was healthy for his serenity. Somehow, he had to find the strength to sleep beside her and keep his hands to himself.

He ran shaky fingers through his hair. "Look, Sky, we need to be on our toes tomorrow. To do that we've got to get some sleep. Which side of the bed do you want?"

She looked as if he'd said she needed surgery without anesthetic. "I—I don't know. I'm used to having the whole thing to myself."

"How about if I take the left side, by the phone? I'm on call this weekend. It could ring anytime—day or night."

"Okay." She swallowed as she gave him a thorough once-over. "Is that all you're wearing? To bed, I mean?"

He glanced at his sweat shorts. "Yeah. It's more than I normally have on."

She nodded. "So—would you mind putting on a T-shirt?"

He grinned. "Okay."

"Would you mind not smiling while you're doing it?"

"I'll do my best."

He pulled a white undershirt from his armoire and put it on. When he turned around, she was in her assigned portion of the bed with the covers pulled up to her chin. He walked to the other side and slid in, then turned off the light. The tension emanating from her was palpable. Along with her sweet, fragrant scent. And her warmth.

"Sky?"

"What?"

"Thank you."

"Why?" she asked, her voice soft, seductive in the dark.

"For not backing out."

"I gave my word."

He let out a long breath. "I'm glad you're here."

"It's the least I could do."

Not by a long shot, he thought. "One more thing."

"Okay."

"During the night, if you find me irresistible, there's something I want you to do."

"What's that?" she asked, a note of wry humor and disbelief in her voice.

"Don't hold back."

He felt her surprise, then she giggled. The bed shook from her laughter. It was contagious and he joined in. For several moments they laughed uncontrollably. He glanced over and in the semidarkness saw her wipe her eyes.

Then she took a deep breath. "Thanks. I needed that."

"You're welcome."

"For the record, now that I've gotten to know you, I don't believe you have a stone heart. And anyone who says different will have to answer to me."

"Thanks." He'd needed that.

"Good night," she said, rolling away, putting her back to him.

"Sleep well," he said, turning his back on her, too.

If only it were that easy to get her out of his mind. He'd meant his remark to disarm her, relax her, ease her tension. But after the words were out, he realized he was only half kidding. Clearly, he needed to get the other half under control.

His mother had said he was impetuous, impatient. She knew him well. He'd jumped into a serious relationship with Shelby, which proved Sky's theory wrong. Dr. StoneHeart didn't know the first thing about love or being in it. Smart men didn't make the same mistake twice, and he was considered by many to be pretty damned intelligent. He would not become involved with Sky Colton.

Just because she was in his bed didn't mean he had to act on his attraction. Make that, acute attraction.

Chapter Eight

Alone in the kitchen, Sky stood at the sink rinsing breakfast dishes before putting them in the dishwasher. She was tired. And not from doing the horizontal hokeypokey. For two days they'd been touching, kissing, cuddling and behaving in a manner to convince the romance police they were in love. After forty-eight hours of this, two nights in his bed had been sheer torture. Not to mention an exercise in self-control that should make any diet a piece of cake by comparison. The irony of the image didn't escape her.

If her situation hadn't been so pathetic, she might have laughed. Maybe she was feeling a little put out because a tiny part of her had hoped he would take his own advice and not hold back. But he hadn't. Apparently she was resistible. So resistible that the man fell asleep faster than you could say hanky-panky, so soundly that he didn't move all night. She should know because she'd been awake most of that time. Breathing in the masculine scent of his skin, listening to him breathe, watching the shadows caress the contours of his wide chest—which in her infinite shortsightedness she'd made him cover with a T-shirt. But it wasn't just his looks. The more she got to know Dominic Rodriguez, the more she liked and respected him.

She couldn't think of many men—correction, *any* man—who would go through such an elaborate scenario to give his mother a gift. His generosity, not to mention his sex appeal and animal magnetism, were becoming increasingly difficult to ignore, let alone resist. In fact, she suspected soon it would be downright impossible.

Sensing someone behind her, she glanced over her shoulder just as Dom slipped his arms around her, nestling her back to his chest. Lord help her. After wishing for this most of the night, it felt good to be held by him. She grew warm from head to toe and a knot of tension tightened low in her belly.

He whispered in her ear, "We have to act like we're in love. Remember?"

"As if I could forget," she said, mimicking his low tone.

He held her snugly against him and bent until she felt his teeth gently nibble her ear. Instantly, tingles skittered over her skin. She sucked in a breath and, instead of pulling away, tipped her head slightly, giving him easier access to her neck—or anything else he wanted. It was the darnedest thing. Whenever he touched her, resistance disappeared. She'd have been a goner if he'd done this in bed. Wow, was she relieved he'd kept his hands to himself. And anyone who bought that piece of fertilizer would believe cubic zirconia was a girl's best friend.

No doubt about it—she needed a break from Dr. Delicious. Thank goodness it was Monday and he would be going to the office.

His linked hands slowly slid up from her abdomen. She held her breath as he stopped just beneath her breasts and brushed his thumbs ever so lightly across the underside. Even through her sweater, she could feel the heat. It was the most erotic sensation she'd ever experienced. Her heart pounded painfully. Thank goodness the doctor was in. If she needed help, he would know what to do.

Now *that* was an understatement. The man definitely knew what to do.

"W-we need to stop," she whispered as he nuzzled his way across her cheek. "It's just you and me. Victoria and your grandmother went upstairs."

"They'll be back any second," he answered, his voice hoarse. "I'm sure of it."

"Right. We have to make this look goo-ood—" She squeaked out the last word as his mouth found the spot on her neck that worked for her in a very big way.

"You like that?" he asked in a seductive whisper.

"It's all right."

He chuckled and the movement of his chest vibrated against her back. "If it's just all right, I guess my technique needs work."

"P-practice makes perfect." Was that wanton whisper coming from her? The last time she'd said that, they'd nearly set her apartment on fire.

"Perfect." His thumbs slowly moved back and forth underneath her breasts. His breath, shallow and uneven, sounded in her ear and stroked her neck. "You are perfect."

"Liar."

But she couldn't deny that he made her want to be. If only she hadn't learned the hard way that she would never come close. Or fit into his life. They were just play-acting. How fortunate for her that he made the act as easy as falling off a log. Still, she couldn't bring herself to end the performance. Not just yet. Not when it felt so good. Just a little longer—

"Are you two at it again?"

That was his grandmother, but there was an amused tone in her voice indicating she approved.

"Mama, isn't young love wonderful?"

"Indeed it is, Victoria. I'm old, but not so ancient I don't remember what it was like with your father."

When Dom stepped back, Sky instantly missed the warmth of his body pressed to hers. She turned toward the two women standing just inside the doorway. As she did, his arm immediately slipped around her waist and pulled her to his side, as if he'd also missed the contact.

She glanced up but found his expression hooded. Slipping her arm around him as if it was the most natural thing in the world, she realized it did feel entirely too easy. This was just pretend, she reminded herself. Don't believe it. Don't buy into the fantasy. It was too darn hard when she started to believe in make-believe. Because the fairy tale would turn on her.

"Dominic," his mother said, "do you go to your office dressed in jeans and a T-shirt? I know for certain you were brought up better than that."

Sky glanced down, not all that surprised she hadn't noticed. He was indeed wearing blue jeans so soft and worn the material clung to the muscles of his thighs like a second skin. Navy cotton molded to the contours of his wide chest. It was a dynamite look, but not what the well-dressed doctor should wear to see patients in the office.

Sky cleared her throat. "Your mother has a point. I didn't notice."

"You were distracted," his grandmother said wryly.

There was an understatement. She looked up at him. "Let me guess. Your doctor duds are at the dry cleaner's?"

He shook his head. "I'm taking the day off."

Uh-oh. "What about your appointments?"

"I had Grace book me light this week. I just phoned in and told her to cancel my patients for today and re-book them. I'm on call, but unless I get a page, I'm all yours."

All hers? A happy glow started in her abdomen. She couldn't stop it any more than she could reverse a tidal wave.

"That's... Wow—" she said. "Why?"

"Because I wanted to spend time with you."

This from the man who couldn't spare the time to buy his former fiancée an engagement ring or pick out wedding bands? Careful, she reminded herself. This wasn't about her. It was all about appearances, about a ruse to do something nice for his mother and grandmother. And visiting with them.

Sky met his gaze. "I don't know what to say."

"How about 'hot dog, that's the best news I've had all day'?" he asked, one eyebrow raised.

"Hot dog, that's the best news I've had all day. But Victoria and Mrs. Castillo made me promise to take them shopping with me for a wedding dress. You don't want to—"

"I'd love to tag along," he said.

Victoria wagged her finger at him. "You can't see her in the dress."

He shrugged. "I'll just go along for the ride. I'll be your chauffeur."

His last fiancée had run off with one, Sky thought.

She saw the glint in his dark eyes and knew he was remembering that, too.

She pulled in a deep breath. ‘‘Well, who knew that tall, dark and handsome loves to shop? You're a tough act for the average man to follow. It just doesn't get any better than that.’’

‘‘You're a lucky girl, Sky,’’ Victoria commented.

‘‘Don't I know it.’’

And if there was a God, her luck wouldn't run out before this was over.

Several hours later Sky walked into the hospital waiting room carrying a tray filled with sandwiches, coffee and soft drinks. Dom had been paged to the E.R.. A fireman, trying to stop a gas leak, had been burned in a flash fire. Sky and the other two women had gone with him to save time. They'd decided if Dom was too long, they would call a taxi to take them home. Instead, they'd found the fireman's family waiting anxiously for word of his condition. Sky's heart had instantly gone out to the mother and her two young children.

When Sky had seen the signs of waiting begin to strain the woman's nerves, she'd gone to the cafeteria. It was all she could think of to help, and she desperately wanted to do something.

The lounge was large, with gray-blue woven material covering the institutional-type chairs around the perimeter. Couches filled the center space with generic tables made of a woodlike substance placed here and there. Muted sound came from a TV mounted on the wall.

‘‘I'll just set this on the coffee table,’’ she said as the swinging door flapped shut behind her. She put the orange plastic tray down in front of the little boy who was on his knees running a toy car along the tabletop. "I've got sandwiches—"

"I only like peanut butter and jelly," four-year-old Jack said.

"Then you're in luck, my friend. I've got one here for you. The hospital chef made it special. Grape jelly. Right?" she asked, her heart breaking for the small boy with white-blond hair.

He nodded solemnly. "Can I have a soda?"

"No caffeine," his mother said. Cathy Martin was a little older than Sky, but not by much. Her straight blond hair and big blue eyes gave her a fragile, waiflike appearance. She held nine-month-old Emily in her arms. They could be models for the Precious Moments figurines. "I don't like him to have too much sugar, either. I'll be peeling him off the walls if he does," she explained.

"I got a carton of milk," Sky said.

"Thanks." She shifted the baby to her hip and started to help her son.

Victoria Rodriguez walked over. "May I hold the baby for you?"

Cathy glanced at the infant. "I'm not sure she'll go to you. But if you'd like to try—"

"I would." Dom's mother held her arms out to the small girl who went to her with only the slightest hesitation. "It will be good training."

"For what?" With her hands now free, the woman knelt on the floor beside the boy and opened the small container of milk.

"My son, Dr. Rodriguez, and Sky are getting married soon. The announcement was in the newspaper this morning," she said proudly.

Cathy looked up at her. "Congratulations."

"Thanks," Sky answered, feeling guilty as all get-out. Wrong thing, right reason, she reminded herself.

Victoria swayed back and forth with the infant in her arms. "I hope to have a grandchild very soon. It's been a long time since I held a little one. So, you see, you're doing me a favor. I need to know if I've lost my touch."

Sky watched the older woman with the baby, who was studying her wide-eyed and a bit wary, but not wailing. "You look like a natural to me."

"I can hardly wait to be a grandmother."

"And I a great-grandmother," Mrs. Castillo interjected. "It would be a nice thing before I die."

At the word, the young mother stood, looking nervous. "What's taking so long? The doctor's been with Johnny for so long. It feels like hours. I can't stand the waiting."

Sky took her arm and steered her away from the boy who was happily eating his sandwich. "I won't lie and tell you I know what's going on. Or that everything will be okay. We'll have to wait and see about that. But I can tell you what I know to be the absolute truth—Dom, Dr. Rodriguez, is the very best at what he does."

"He's a burn specialist?"

Sky nodded. "Actually a plastic surgeon—"

"He gave Sky new boobs," Mrs. Castillo chimed in.

Cathy's gaze automatically went to her chest and Sky said, "You thought they'd be bigger."

A smile curved the other woman's mouth. "Yeah."

"I get that a lot."

"I guess so," Cathy agreed.

"Dom is a plastic surgeon who specializes in burns," Sky continued.

Mrs. Castillo moved closer and studied her, a skeptical

expression in her dark eyes. "I thought you didn't like hospitals."

"I don't especially."

"Me, either," Cathy said.

"But you told me you didn't want anything to do with Dom's work because of it. That you couldn't stand to see people in pain. You would faint at the sight of blood. You can't understand how he does what he does."

"That's true," she said, feeling cornered. Again. "But since we tagged along with him, I have to do something. Even though it doesn't seem to matter."

Cathy's small smile was trimmed with worry. "It matters. A lot."

"I'm glad." Sky pointed to the tray of sandwiches. "Are you hungry? I bought a ham and cheese, turkey and mayo, roast beef. I didn't know what you liked."

"Thanks, but I don't think I could eat a thing."

Sky couldn't blame her. If Dom—if someone she loved was in the same situation, she didn't know if she could be as calm as Cathy Martin. It gave her a new respect for the courageous families and heroic firemen. They were the first ones called to the rescue when someone needed help. Sky had always taken it for granted that training kept them safe. Today she'd learned that wasn't always the case. The least she could do was support this young woman and her children as best she could.

Behind her the doors swung open and she whirled to see Dom in the doorway. He'd changed out of his jeans and T-shirt. Now he wore green surgical scrubs under a white lab coat. She made a mental note to tease him later about his fashion accessories. He had a stethoscope draped around his neck and it didn't do a thing for the ensemble. But her heart caught at the lines of weariness bracketing his nose and mouth.

Cathy rushed toward him. "Doctor, how is Johnny?"

"He's in serious condition, Mrs. Martin. He's burned over forty percent of his body."

"Oh, God," she said, putting a hand over her mouth.

Without a word, Sky moved forward and put her arm around the woman's shoulders. She didn't know any other way to show her support.

Dom looked at her then at his patient's wife as he ran a hand through his hair. "He has third-degree burns on his hands, arms and face. We took him to surgery."

"Surgery?" Cathy echoed, fear clinging to every syllable.

"It was necessary to debride the areas—that means we cleaned the burns to keep them from getting infected. It's an extremely painful procedure and best done under anesthesia in a sterile environment." He let out a long breath. "Infection presents the most imminent danger. So we cover the wounds to minimize the possibility. We used synthetic skin on some burns, cream and bandages on the less serious areas."

"Is he going to be all right?"

"Barring anything unforeseen," he said cautiously. "We got to him fast. He's young and in excellent physical condition. The odds are definitely in his favor."

Jack walked over and took his mother's hand as he looked up at Dom. "Are you gonna make my daddy well?"

Dom went down on one knee, to the boy's level. "I'm going to do my best."

"Did you give him a shot?" the child asked solemnly.

"Yes."

"When I get shots at the doctor's it hurts. I don't like shots."

"Your dad got medicine to make his pain go away," Dom said simply.

"I got burned once," the boy said. "On the Fourth of July I touched a sparkler even though Daddy said not to. I cried. I got a blister."

Dom nodded. "It hurts a lot. Because of the shot, your dad's feeling a lot better now."

The little boy threw his arms around Dom's neck. "I'm glad you gave my daddy a shot."

"You bet, buddy." He rubbed his large hand up and down over the small back.

Sky remembered thinking how much she liked Dom's hands. Hands that evoked passion. Magic hands. Healing hands.

"May I see my husband now?" Cathy asked.

"You can go in—alone—for a few minutes," he said, standing.

Sky squeezed her arm. "We'll watch the children. Victoria has the baby wrapped around her finger. And Mrs. Castillo and I—"

"It's Isabel," the older woman said beside her.

Sky felt a glow start deep inside and thought surely it must show. Unexpectedly, her eyes burned with tears and emotion lodged in her throat. "Thank you, Isabel," she managed to say. She looked at Cathy. "We can handle Jack."

"Are you sure?"

Sky nodded. "Take as long as you need."

"Before you go in, Mrs. Martin, I need to explain what to expect," Dom said. "Your husband is sedated so he can rest and heal. He's got an IV to hydrate him and prevent shock. He's on a respirator to help him breathe while his lungs heal from smoke damage. All of the equipment and tubes look scary, but it's there to help him get better. Don't be afraid. Talk to him. I'm convinced even under sedation patients somehow know when the people who love them are there."

Cathy nodded. "Thank you, Doctor. For everything."

"You're welcome. Ask at the information desk for directions to the burn unit."

Sky watched the young woman nod, then hurry through the swinging doors. Then she looked up at Dom. She'd seen him in action when the fireman had been brought in. Nurses and respiratory therapists had reacted instantly when he gave orders. All of the hospital personnel treated him with awe and respect. But it was as if an invisible force field separated him from them. Dr. StoneHeart. His manner was professional yet reserved. Certainly different from the man she shared a bed with, the man who had told her not to hold back if she found him irresistible.

Sky moved close to him and stood on tiptoe to put her arms around his neck.

"Is this part of the act?" he asked, a slight tone of regret in his voice. But before she could answer, he slipped his arms around her in return. Then he made a sound—half sigh, half moan—and his hold on her tightened, almost desperately.

"No. You just looked like a man in need of a hug."

His only answer was a sigh as he rested his cheek against her hair. He gave of himself, everything he had. He was available twenty-four seven, to use his special skill to save lives. But sometimes his skill wasn't enough. She remembered his story about the little girl he'd lost and knew that wasn't easy for him to accept. When it happened, who did he turn to? Who was there for him? Who filled up his emotional well when it ran dry because he'd used up everything he had?

He'd almost had Shelby. But the more she learned from Dom's grandmother about his ex-fiancée, the more relieved she was that the wedding wouldn't happen.

He loosened his hold and stared with great intensity into her eyes. "I'm glad you stayed."

"Me, too." She glanced over her shoulder at his mother, who was cooing to the baby. "Your mom wants to be a grandmother."

"That's not a news flash." He grinned.

Sky smiled back, glad to see the spark of humor that was happening more often. "Under different circumstances this could get really complicated. You should be glad I'm impersonating your fiancée instead of your wife."

"I should be," he agreed, his eyes darkening as he studied her. "Do you like children?"

"Yes," she said. "Do you?"

"Very much."

That revelation and the tender way he'd talked to his patient's little boy made Sky wonder why a fondness for kids hadn't been one of the qualifications he'd listed for his wife. Not to mention love. But he hadn't mentioned either. What was that about?

"I have to go check on my patient. You don't have to wait."

She recalled him telling her that when he got called in for a burn victim, everything else stopped. He stayed with the patient until he was stable, which could take all day.

"I know," she said. "When Mrs. Martin comes back, I'll take your mother and grandmother home. But I think

I'll come back. To see if there's anything I can do to help."

"Okay. I'll see you as soon as I can."

The look in his eyes was fierce, as if he didn't want to go. But it was more, as if he was drawing strength straight from her. Then he bent and touched his lips to hers, a tender caress that, oddly enough, returned what he'd taken. And then some.

When he left, she thought his step was a bit lighter. The idea that she'd put a little sunshine back in his heart made her feel good. Really useful, as if she'd done something important.

What a time to realize she was playing with fire. He'd joked about her finding him irresistible. It wasn't funny anymore. He'd said she shouldn't hold back. God knew she didn't want to. But what else could she do? He was on the rebound, and she wasn't the girl his mother thought she was—the one who Dom had thought would be perfect for him. Somehow she had to find the strength to fulfill her part of this bargain, then move on.

Preferably with her heart in one large attractive piece.

Chapter Nine

"Ladies and gentlemen—" Dom tapped on his champagne glass for attention. Everyone who was coming had arrived and it was time to get this engagement party going. "I have an announcement to make."

Standing behind a table at the front of the room, he looked down at Sky and suddenly couldn't breathe, she was so punch-to-the-gut beautiful. The simple, long-sleeved, scoop-necked, knee-length, lacy little black dress she wore clung to her body in a way that should be illegal. The womanly curves made his fingers itch to thoroughly explore each and every one. Admittedly, his reaction could be a heightened response caused by sleeping beside her for the past week without the right to touch her. Which would be his own damn fault. What the hell had he been thinking?

Obviously he hadn't. But it was high time he started. Because this engagement party was the culmination of everything he and Sky had worked for.

He'd reserved a banquet room in one of Houston's

most exclusive restaurants for the occasion. Sky had picked things up from there—deciding on a dinner menu, the arrangement of circular tables around the room with a rectangular one in front, an abundance of flowers and candles for centerpieces, music for dancing, keeping track of who had RSVPed for the final number of expected guests.

Without his ex-fiancée's friends and acquaintances, the gathering was quite a bit smaller than it would otherwise have been. The guests were seated around the tables watching him intently while waiters poured champagne. As he looked out at the faces, he noticed Grace and her boyfriend Rob. There were doctors, some nurses and a few others from the hospital. His mother and grandmother stood close by, beaming.

"Everyone, I guess you're curious about the reason I've gathered you together." A collective chorus of assent rose up from the onlookers. He curved his arm around Sky's slender waist, pulling her close. Something about having her there felt so right. Ignoring the sensation, he continued. "I have an announcement to make. This beautiful lady—best known to her friends as Sky—has become more than a friend to me. I asked her to be my wife and I'm delighted to say she accepted."

"You should have told us this was an engagement party," somebody shouted.

Sky put her hand on his suit jacket, over his heart. "We wanted it to be a surprise."

"But we'd have brought presents," a woman said.

"We don't want gifts. Your shocked expressions are gift enough," Sky said, smiling.

"No, it's not." Victoria stepped to his other side.

She opened her small evening purse and pulled something out. When she held it up, he saw it was a ring.

"Dom's father gave me this when he proposed. Since Dom hasn't gotten around to picking out an engagement ring for his fiancée, I want Sky to have it."

Dom heard her gasp and felt her body stiffen. He looked down and met her stormy gray gaze. "What is it?"

"Do something," Sky whispered. "I can't take a ring. It's your mother's."

His mother frowned. "Sky, is something wrong?"

"No. I just—Wow."

"You surprised us, Mama. I think my bride-to-be is speechless for maybe the first time since I've known her." The remark elicited laughter from the gathering.

His mother looked doubtful. "Speechless is okay, but Sky looks like she's going to cry."

Dom glanced down. There were indeed tears swimming in her eyes. He'd seen her angry, annoyed, caring, concerned, teasing and turned on. But he'd never seen her look the way she did now, as if she were going to cry. He hated it. Worse, he didn't know how to fix it. Maybe whoever had first called him StoneHeart was right. His chest tightened and felt as though it was pulling apart, like a crevice opening.

"She's just happy," he said lamely.

His mother held out the ring and he saw it was an emerald. Sky's favorite color.

"Put it on," Victoria said to him.

"No." Sky shook her head. "I can't accept this."

"But why? I want you to have it."

"It's too much. Your husband gave it to you and you should keep it as a token of his love. I don't need a ring."

The woman stared fondly at her. "I don't need a token. I carry his love here," she said, putting her hand over her heart. ‘‘And here,’’ she said pressing a finger to her temple. ‘‘I want the woman my son is going to marry to have something that represents the love of his parents.’’

Dom took her hand and slipped it onto her left ring finger. ‘‘Fits perfectly,’’ he commented.

The gaze she turned up to his was bleak. ‘‘How about that?’’

Dom picked up his flute with the bubbling liquid and handed Sky hers. He looked out at their guests. ‘‘Champagne has been served and everyone should have a glass by now. I’d like to make a toast. To Sky, my bride, my support, my everything.’’

The words had come surprisingly easily and were simple. The feelings they evoked were anything but. Because it felt like the truth. But how could that be?

A chorus rose from the gathering, ‘‘To Sky and Dominic.’’ Then there was a loud tinkling sound as the guests touched glasses and drank.

Dom clinked with Sky, then his mother and grandmother. After sealing it with a sip, he looked out over the guests. ‘‘Thanks for coming. Dinner will be served soon. After that we have music and dancing. As you all know, I don’t tolerate slackers. I want everyone to get up and dance. Sky and I want you all to have a good time tonight.’’

Afterward, Dom was swept up in a blur of hand shaking and congratulations. It was a while before he realized Sky had slipped away to a table in the far corner. He joined her in the shadows.

‘‘What’s wrong?’’ he asked, sitting beside her, their backs to the room.

‘‘How can you ask me that? It should be obvious.’’

She held out her hand and stared at the ring on her finger. "I feel like a criminal."

"Do you want to know something?"

After several moments she turned her stormy gray gaze up to his. "What?"

"I do, too."

"Sweet of you to say, but not especially helpful. When I agreed to help you, I never figured on this. I've fallen in love with—" She stopped and her eyes widened before she huffed out a breath and looked away.

"What?"

"I've fallen for your family. They're completely wonderful. Although I do wish Isabel would stop telling everyone that you gave me new boobs."

"I'll talk to her."

"What's the point? Tomorrow they leave on the cruise. Then you'll be home free."

And she would go home. As in gone and he wouldn't see her again. His heart of stone cracked some more.

"Yeah." He put his hand on hers, stilling her nervous movements as she plucked at the white-linen tablecloth. He lifted her hand in his to gaze at the ring on her finger. The one his father had given his mother. It was set in gold, the emerald's green color winking through the filigree in the setting. Somehow it looked right and perfect on her.

Sky curled her fingers into the palm of her hand. "This is so much harder than I thought it would be. I have to tell you, I'm glad this ruse is almost over. By this time tomorrow I'll be back in Black Arrow and you'll—"

"Be trying to figure out how to tell my mother that there's not going to be a wedding when she gets back from her trip." He glanced over his shoulder and saw his relatives talking to Grace and her boyfriend. "I've never seen her so happy. I don't want to think about how she's going to feel when I break the news to her."

"No grandchildren," she said, a little sadly.

"Are you sorry about that?"

A small smile curved her full lips. "We would have had beautiful babies. If we weren't pretending to be in love."

"Yeah. If."

Dom was having trouble figuring out what pretend meant when what he was feeling seemed real enough to produce physical sensations. For a man of science and logic, he was fresh out of reasonable explanations for it. In his work, he'd seen the occasional miracle. But by and large, diagnosis and treatment ruled his medical career, a series of decisions based on grueling study, gut reactions generated by experience and intense training.

Unfortunately none of his training included instruction on relationships. Nothing in his experience explained sufficiently why his feelings for Sky Colton weren't going away. God forbid he should have a clue about the sudden pain in his chest when she'd reminded him that this time tomorrow she would be gone.

He was a doctor, for Pete's sake. Pain was the result of a physical anomaly. It was not a consequence of emotion.

Dom felt a hand on his shoulder and looked up. "Hey, *Abuelita.*"

She smiled. "Shame on you, Dominic. What are you doing hiding in the corner and looking so serious?"

"Just taking a break," Sky volunteered. "We'll need our energy when the dancing starts."

"Not because you are feeling sad that your parents are not here?"

"That's part of it, I guess. They picked a bad time to go on a business trip." That and the fact that most of her friends lived too far away were the lies they'd prepared to explain why only his family and friends were in attendance.

Isabel looked at her, a fond expression softening her wrinkled face. "The other part, I think, is you are in love and wishing to be alone."

"That, too," Sky agreed, starting to stand. "But you're right. We should return to our guests."

"Wait." The older woman put a hand on her shoulder, settling her back on the chair. "Before you go shake your booty, or whatever it is you young people call dancing these days, there is something I would like to say to you."

"What is it?" Sky glanced at him, an uneasy look pulling her lips into a straight line.

"When Dominic told me he was going to marry a rich oilman's daughter, my Victoria was thrilled. 'Just like the lovely ladies I have worked for,' she said. 'For once he has listened to his mama,' she said. But I was not so sure you were the right one for him. Especially after reading those electronic letters you sent me. I did not think you would suit my grandson."

"I'm sorry you—"

Isabel touched a finger to Sky's lips to shush her. "I was wrong."

"Really?" She glanced at him, her expression a mixture of misery and guilt.

"Since meeting you, I have seen a beautiful young woman who thinks of others first. Dominic is different with you."

"How?" Sky asked, curiosity chasing away her frown.

"He jokes. He teases. He smiles. He's happy. He looks at you the way his father looked at his mother when he was courting her."

"How?" she asked again.

"As if she was responsible for the moon, the sun and the stars in the sky." She laughed. "It's no wonder he calls you Sky. I am delighted to say I was quite mistaken about you, my dear. Victoria and I can go away on our trip tomorrow and know that our boy is in good hands. Most important, he is well and truly loved."

"I'm glad you'll go away with a clear mind," Sky said, her bleak look returning.

The older woman kissed her cheek. "And now Victoria and I have a surprise for you. Look," she said, pointing to the front of the room.

A busboy was setting up an easel. On it he set a sort of canvas, an eleven-by-fourteen-inch picture of the two of them.

Sky looked at it, then him. "That's the photograph we had taken and put in the newspaper."

His grandmother smiled, obviously excited about the surprise. "Victoria had it blown up. Tonight all your guests will be invited to sign your engagement picture. Later we will have it framed as a memento of this night when you announced your marriage." Glancing at the picture and back at Sky, she sighed. "See the way you look at my grandson, with so much love. When did you first know he is the one you will be with forever?"

"This is too much." The tears swimming in Sky's eyes spilled over and trickled down her cheeks. She stood and hugged his grandmother, then excused herself and left the room.

"What did I say?"

"Nothing, *Abuelita.* She's just feeling—"

"Happy?"

He'd bet his medical license that wasn't the case. "I need to go—"

"Yes, you do," she said.

Sky hurried through the restaurant and past the ladies' room to a rear exit. She pushed open the door and a blast of cold January air hit her. All but tumbling into the dimly lit parking lot, she let the door close behind her. As she walked away from the building, she dragged air into her lungs then let it out, making a white cloud in front of her face. Darkness closed in around her. Cars filled the lot on this busy Saturday night. Cars and shadows.

It took several moments for her hot cheeks to cool. How could she have lied to those two wonderful women? It didn't matter that Dom had put her up to it, or that he believed there was a good reason. Ultimately the decision had been her own. And the consequences were hers, too.

She'd lied!

She'd pretended to be the perfect woman. They accepted her. They embraced her as one of the family. They believed she and Dom were in love. They would be half-right.

"When did I know I loved him?" she said softly. "That would be now."

"Well, well."

Sky turned to her left, toward the sound. There was a spotlight just above the restaurant exit door, but the voice came from the shadows beyond it, next to the building. She could only see the outline of a man and the burning red tip of his cigarette.

"Who's there?" she asked, her knees starting to shake.

"An old friend of the family." The red glow arced through the air as he tossed the cigarette between two parked cars.

Then his heels clicked on the asphalt as he moved forward, toward her, into the circle of light. He stopped, just out of reach. Sky squinted, trying to see, to make out his features. He was average-looking. Average height, average clothes. His hair was brown and she couldn't tell about his eyes although they looked dark. He looked familiar. She'd seen him someplace before. But where?

"You know my family?"

"Yeah. If it isn't Sky Colton."

He said her last name with such loathing, she suddenly knew and her blood turned cold.

"Kenny Randolph."

Chapter Ten

Sky backed away. Good Lord. She'd been so caught up in her overwhelming feelings for Dom and their deception, she'd completely forgotten the threat Kenny Randolph was to herself and her family. She had to get back inside—to Dom. But Kenny was between her and the door. Before she could do anything, he grabbed her. The grin of satisfaction on his face sent fear slicing down her spine.

"Fancy meeting you," he said.

He smiled. If possible, the deceptively friendly look frightened her more. He'd hurt her cousin Willow in his search for information to cheat the Oklahoma Coltons out of their rightful inheritance. Her family had been living with the threat of him for too long. It was time to stop the fear, stop him. But how? She was alone. Unless someone at the party missed her, she was on her own.

Dom, please miss me, she prayed.

"What a coincidence. Kenny Randolph." Not letting fear show was a defense against some animals. Anyone who did the things he had was definitely an animal. But it took every ounce of backbone Sky had to keep her voice steady and return his stare. ''What are you doing in Houston?''

''I needed to disappear for a while. Dallas is too close to Black Arrow for my peace of mind. Houston is the fourth largest city in the country. Did you know that?''

''While I appreciate the geography lesson, I'd appreciate it more if you'd let me go.'' She tugged against his hold.

''I don't think so.'' He squeezed her wrist harder. ''You're just the person I was looking for.''

''How did you know I was here?''

''Your mother.''

''She wouldn't tell you anything,'' Sky said, trying to pull free, but he tightened his grip until it felt as if he would snap her bones.

''She didn't know it was me. I pretended to be a jewelry designer friend and needed your help. She was very helpful and told me I could get in touch with you through the doc. Finding out where he lived was easy. I've been following you for a couple days, just waiting for a chance to make my move.''

''What do you want?''

''The same thing I've always wanted—money.''

''Try working for a living,'' she snapped.

''I worked for Graham Colton until he lost his nerve. There's no loyalty anymore. I work hard and look how I wind up. Your family owes me. And I'm going to collect—one way or the other.''

''We owe you nothing, you lowlife creep. What are you talking about?''

''That inheritance that Graham thinks should be his. I bet your family would give it up to get you back.''

He was planning to kidnap her. She thought of Dom and her newly discovered love. And the fact that she might never know what could have been. Frustration and fear gathered inside her and she struggled to hold back the threatening panic. She needed to do something. She couldn't just let him get away with this—not without a fight.

"If you're smart you'll let me go. My family won't pay you a red cent. And they won't rest until you're locked up."

"I'm willing to risk it," he said, dragging her toward him.

"Then you're a fool."

She heard the door open and prayed it was help.

Kenny jerked on her arm, pulling her up against his chest. "You're just like the rest of the Coltons. High and mighty. Holier than thou. Let me tell you, Sky Colton—"

"Let her go."

"Dom." Her legs nearly buckled from relief.

"This is between her and me," Kenny said, whirling her around so that her back was to his front.

He tugged her away from the building, farther into the parking lot. The only thing that kept her on her feet was the sight of Dom highlighted beneath the spotlight above the door. She drew strength from him.

"Let her go," Dom repeated, his deep voice as unbending as steel. His eyes burned with rage. Determination tightened his jaw. "Go call the police," he said over his shoulder to someone behind him that she couldn't see.

Light spilling out from inside the restaurant was cut off as the door closed. Kenny jerked her again, farther away from Dom. The creep must have a car close by.

He was trying to get to it—with her. She tried to halt their progress by digging in her heels. Four-inch black satin pumps didn't grip asphalt.

"Don't mess with me," Kenny hissed. "If you know what's good for you, you'll go quietly."

"Right back at you," she said.

He yanked her backward, wrenching her arm up behind her and she cried out.

"Sky!" Dom shouted, anger and alarm mixed together in his tone. "Let her go, you bastard. If you hurt her I'll—"

As they crept steadily backward her foot hit a pebble and slid out from under her. High-heeled pumps also had no stability and her ankle twisted sideways. The wrenching jolt made her cry out as she lost her footing. The sudden movement surprised Kenny and made him lose his hold on her as she went down. Sharp pain shot through her ankle and lower leg, then back up to her knee. The next thing she knew, Dom was there. He grabbed Kenny's shirt and dragged him away from her. Then he pulled his arm back, his fingers curled into his palm.

"No, Dom. Your hand. Don't!"

The words were barely out of her mouth when he smashed his fist into Kenny's face. The other man took a swing and caught Dom's cheek, snapping his head back. Dom hit him again, a right, then a left. Kenny groaned, then crumpled onto the asphalt.

Sirens whined in the distance as Dom dropped to one knee beside her.

"Are you all right?" He took her arms and lifted her to her feet.

"I'm fine," she answered, then winced as she put weight on the ankle.

"Liar." With his arm encircling her waist, he took most of her weight. Then he moved the fingers on his right hand, as if he was in pain.

"Oh, gosh." She took his big hand between her smaller ones and inspected it. "Is anything broken?"

"No. Don't worry about it."

"Yeah, like that's going to happen." How could she not worry when she loved him so?

But after tonight, he would do the dance of joy when she walked out of his life tomorrow. Her teeth started to chatter from cold and delayed reaction. Dom released her to remove his suit coat and slipped it around her shoulders. Sky pulled the edges together and savored the warmth from his body and the scent of his skin. It only made her want to be in his arms.

The next instant police cars with lights flashing and sirens wailing screeched into the parking lot. Uniformed officers surrounded them and it took several moments to explain the situation.

Sky instructed them to contact her cousin Bram Colton, and was told he was already on the way. People started to spill out of the restaurant, curious about the commotion, but an officer went inside to keep the looky-loos away. Maybe things weren't as bad as she thought. It was possible no one at the party knew what was going on.

"Miss Colton." A uniform officer looked down at her. "We'd like you to come down to the station and wait for Sheriff Colton."

"Do I have to?" she asked.

"The sheriff requested we keep you in protective custody until he gets there."

"That's not necessary, is it?"

"If you were my family I would do the same thing," the man said.

"Okay." Sky glanced from Dom to the policeman. "Officer, this is Dr. Dominic Rodriguez. He punched out the perp and needs to have his hand looked at."

"It's fine," Dom said, obviously aggravated. "And I'm going with you."

"But what about your mother and grandmother?"

"I'll make sure they get home."

The officer met his gaze. "We'll take Miss Colton to the station. You can meet us there."

Frowning, he looked at her and hesitated. "I'm not letting you out of my sight. I'll have Grace and her boyfriend take care of them."

"Okay." A glow started inside her at his words, but Sky stopped it cold. He was a man who took his responsibilities seriously. That's all this was about. He walked toward the restaurant, then stopped and watched as a cuffed Kenny was read his rights and put in a cruiser. "I'll be right back," he said to her.

"What about the party?" she asked, feeling a distance from him so much wider than the few feet separating them.

"They can still have one—without us."

Dom studied Sky across the table from him. The cops had put them in a room that was probably a step up from the interrogation area. The table was metal, the chairs gray plastic. Occasionally a condensation drip from the coffeepot on an old wooden table in the corner hit the heating element and hissed. Packets of cups, condiments and plastic stirrers were neatly arranged beside it. Overhead, fluorescent lights glared down. Law enforcement didn't spend money, time or energy on five-star comforts.

Fortunately they'd only been there a short time, but Sky was still wearing his jacket. She looked so small, so fragile, so young. And he was anxious to get her home. The feeling of protectiveness for her was becoming familiar. He'd first experienced it in Black Arrow's burned courthouse. Now the urgency to care for her flared bright and hot as he studied her pale cheeks, the lingering fear in her eyes. The knot in his gut tightened. He wanted to hit that bastard again for what he'd done to her—and to hell with his hand.

Thank God he'd gone to look for her. He didn't want to think about what could have happened if he hadn't followed when he did. What had made her run outside?

"Sky, I—"

The door opened and she glanced at the man who walked in. "Bram!" She stood.

"Sky."

Limping several steps, she went to the tall, athletic man in the doorway. He caught her in his arms and hugged her, his size and bulk making her seem even smaller, more fragile.

"I'm so glad you're here." Sky's voice was muffled against his chest.

"Are you all right?" His fingers curved around her shoulders as he held her away from him, inspecting her again. He frowned when his gaze took in her ripped nylons, scraped knee and swollen ankle. Turning her hand, his gaze darkened when he saw the bruises on the inside of her wrist. "That son of a—"

"I'm fine. Really. Thanks to Dom," she said, glancing over her shoulder.

Dom walked around the table, holding out his hand to the other man. ''Sheriff.''

''George WhiteBear was right again. There was danger in the big city.'' Bram glared at him. ''How could you let that creep get his hands on her?''

''If I could change what happened, I would,'' Dom said grimly.

Sky put her hand on her cousin's arm. ''Bram, I ran outside— I mean, I went out for some air and Kenny was just there. It's not Dom's fault.''

''Yes, it is,'' Dom said. ''If she'd stayed in Black Arrow like her brother Jesse said, she would have been safe. I'm responsible for putting her in harm's way. I convinced her to come to Houston.''

''Why?'' Bram asked, eyes narrowing.

''That's not important.'' Sky looked from Dom to her cousin. ''I'm fine. But you two look like you're planning intentional infliction of bodily harm. Can we take the testosterone level down a notch or two?''

''Why should I?'' Bram ran a hand through his dark hair as he looked at her.

She smiled. ''Dom saved me. If it hadn't been for him—I don't know what would have happened. The good news is Kenny's in custody.''

''Yeah. I plan to escort him back to Black Arrow personally.''

She eyed him critically. ''You're out of uniform.''

''I was in a hurry.''

Dom noticed his worn boots, jeans, long-sleeved plaid shirt and brown leather jacket. He didn't look like law enforcement. Maybe undercover. Vice.

''That reminds me,'' she said. ''Why are you here?''

''Graham Colton called the Houston police and tipped them off about Kenny's whereabouts. Then he called me and I put the word out to the rest of the family. That's when your mom remembered a call from a man who claimed to be a designer colleague of yours—''

''Kenny told me. He knows about the inheritance money. He was planning to kidnap me for it.''

''Yeah. We called your cell number but you weren't picking up. Houston P.D. dispatched a unit to the doc's, but no one was home.'' His expression turned grimmer, if possible.

Dom knew how he felt. If he hadn't gotten to Sky when he did— The consequences were unthinkable. He couldn't stand the thought of her in danger.

Sky studied her cousin critically. ''What else is up, Bram?''

''You think a near kidnapping isn't enough?''

''That's not what I meant. What's up with you?''

He shifted his feet then put his hands on his hips and met her gaze. ''I don't like being away from Jenna.''

''That's his new wife,'' Sky explained.

''The nurse you told me about,'' Dom clarified.

''Yeah. I'm surprised you remembered.'' She smiled and cocked her thumb in his direction as she looked at the sheriff. ''He's not just another pretty face.''

''If you say so.'' Bram met his gaze but there was no softening in his expression.

''So why don't you like being away from Jenna? Aside from the fact that you adore her,'' Sky asked.

At her words Dom felt a twinge of envy for the other man. He had a special woman waiting at home. Sky had given him a glimpse of what that was all about.

''How do you know there's another reason I'm not dancing with joy at being away from home?'' Bram asked her.

She tipped her head, studying him. "Hey, cousin. This is me. I can just tell. There's something up. What is it?"

"Jenna's pregnant."

"A baby?" Sky's big gray eyes grew wider. Her mouth dropped open and she clapped her hands. Then she launched herself into his arms. "That's wonderful! Congratulations."

"Thanks," he mumbled.

When he set her on her feet, she winced.

"You need to sit," Dom ordered. "And elevate your foot."

He took her arm as she hopped the single step to one of the institutional chairs and lowered herself into it. Then he cupped his hand behind her heel and lifted, setting her foot on the seat of another chair.

Bram frowned. "That creep is going to pay. Besides the fact that he's already a convicted felon, we've got a stack of charges against him that would choke a horse. He'll stand trial for everything he did."

"As lovely as that thought is, I would rather talk about something else," Sky said.

"Like what?"

"Babies."

Again Dom envied the other man. He had someone to go home to and soon there would be another little someone. A baby, the tangible result of their love. Hell, how would he know anything about that? What did he know about love?

How did a man *know* he'd found the right woman? When did he realize she was the one he was meant to be with forever?

"What about babies?" Bram asked.

"How do you feel about becoming a father?" she asked, smiling up at him.

Dom knew exactly how *he* would feel—Sky high.

The other man let out a long breath as he rested his hands on his hips. "How do I feel? It would be easier to describe the taste of sourdough bread."

She laughed. "Are you excited? Scared? Worried? Overwhelmed?"

"All of the above. It's a serious proposition becoming a father. Can I do the job? Changing diapers. How do we know if he or she hurts or is hungry?"

"You'll know," Dom said wryly.

The other man met his gaze and there was a subtle easing of tension in his expression. "What does a plastic surgeon know about kids?"

"I've done a little bit of everything," Dom said. "Even delivered a baby or two in my time."

"No kidding?" Bram said, a note of respect creeping into his voice. "How was it?"

"The scariest thing I've ever done."

"Thanks. I feel a lot better now," the other man said, grinning.

"You'll be fine," Sky assured him. "Babies are the best. How's Jenna feeling?"

"A little green. A lot emotional. She's not eating much and she cries at songs on the radio." He sighed. "I wish I could make it perfect for her."

"You do. Just by being you," Sky said softly.

"You're pretty special," Bram said. "George WhiteBear always said you were the one full of promise."

"He never told me," she said softly.

Her cousin shrugged. "You know how he is, but that doesn't make him less right. And if Kenny had hurt you, I swear, there's nowhere he could hide."

Dom knew how Bram felt. The sight of Sky in danger

earlier that night had scared the life out of him. His blood ran cold at the thought of her at the mercy of that creep Kenny.

"I'm safe. Because of Dom," she said. "The least you could do is say thanks."

"Is there any special reason you're defending him?"

Dom was wondering the same thing. Her gaze briefly rested on him, but shuttered before he could read it.

"Other than the fact he saved my life?" She sighed as she met her cousin's gaze. "Aren't we finished with all this? I'd like to get out of here."

Bram nodded. "You're free to go. I'll take you back to Black Arrow with me."

"I can't go yet. I have some unfinished business here."

Sky looked at him and Dom knew she meant to follow through on her promise to him.

"I want to look at your knee and ankle now."

Dom waited beside the supplies he'd retrieved from the medicine cabinet in the bedroom. Antiseptic, antibiotic cream and bandages were lined up on the kitchen island. He'd turned on the lights in the work area only, leaving the rest of the room dark. No doubt to keep from disturbing his relatives sleeping upstairs.

Limping, Sky walked over to the table. She slid his suit jacket from her shoulders and over the back of a chair. Then she moved to where he waited for her.

He'd loosened his tie and rolled the long sleeves of his white dress shirt to just below his elbows. There was a serious expression on his face and she wondered what he was thinking. He'd hardly said a word on the drive from the police station.

"I'll show you my boo-boo if you let me look at yours," she offered.

"It's nothing."

"That's what all the macho guys say. But they're not the best plastic surgeon in Houston."

He hesitated briefly, then held out his hand. Sky took it between hers. The knuckles were scraped raw and swollen.

"Oh, Dom," she said, cradling his fist between her hands. "Does it hurt? Are you okay? I have brothers. I know about a boxer's fracture. It's the direct result of too much testosterone and not enough common sense. One minute you've got a knuckle, then bam. You hit something—a chin, nose, cheek or block wall, and the knuckle disappears."

"It's fine."

"Are you sure. Is it broken? What about surgery?"

"See? Five knuckles. Count 'em." He moved his fingers to show they all worked. "It's fine."

"You need some ice on it."

"Okay. And the sooner you let me disinfect your scrapes, the sooner I can do that."

"You don't need to doctor me. I can take care of it." She started to limp toward the refrigerator for ice when she felt his hand on her arm.

"I want to make sure the abrasions don't get infected." He put his hands at her waist and lifted, easily setting her on the island. "Presto. Exam table."

"Okay. I'll go first." Her hands rested on his shoulders for balance and she was reluctant to remove them. His blue eyes darkened as his gaze met hers.

Then he was all business, cutting away her torn nylon from just above her knee. He rolled it down her calf and over her foot. His fingers tickled her flesh at the same time he tantalized. Before she quite recovered, he soaked a piece of gauze in hydrogen peroxide and dabbed it on several cuts and scratches on her knee.

"Yikes," she gasped, sucking in a breath.

"Sting?" he asked, his gaze meeting hers, dark and intense.

She nodded. "And cold."

"I can fix that."

He put his palms on the countertop beside her thighs and bent at the waist to blow lightly on the wet area. His breath cooled and soothed even as it fired her blood and agitated her senses.

"Better?" he asked.

She caught the corner of her lip between her teeth and nodded. "Am I going to live?"

She hoped for a smile, and was disappointed when he didn't say anything. "What is it, Dom? You've hardly said two words to me since we left the restaurant. Is it what happened with Kenny? I'm sorry about the party—"

"Forget the party."

She blinked at him. He'd never talked that way before and his vehemence, not to mention the depth of emotion in his voice, shocked her. "I don't understand—"

"You could have been killed. That bastard swore vengeance on your family. If anything had happened to you—" Tension tightened his jaw.

"This is about what Bram said. You blame yourself. Don't—"

"If there was someone else to pin this on I would. But there's just me."

"That's ridiculous."

"Is it? You would have been safe in Black Arrow.

But I couldn't leave it alone. I had to talk you into coming to Houston."

"Did you know Kenny was here?"

"Of course not."

"Then just how is this your fault?" She met his gaze. "It's a coincidence, a lucky one as it turns out. What if he'd found me on his terms, when I was alone? Or if he'd stalked someone else in the family? But you were there."

"Yeah." He ran a hand through his hair. "You were upset at the party." He picked up her hand and gently traced the bruises on the inside of her wrist. Then he stared at the emerald still on her finger. "Green is your favorite color."

She pulled away. "If we're taking on undeserved guilt, I've got some, too. What if you'd damaged your hand? What if you could never do surgery again? How do you think I'd feel about that?"

"Bad?" One corner of his mouth lifted.

"Bad? Is that the best you can do?" She shook her head. "You're a master of understatement."

Suddenly all the kitchen lights went on. Dressed in her robe and slippers, Victoria stood just inside the doorway. She looked anxious.

"Dominic? Sky?"

"It's all right, Mama. We're fine. Go back to bed. You need your rest. Tomorrow is a big day. Your trip—"

"I'm not going anywhere. Will someone please explain to me why that man called your fiancée Sky Colton?"

Chapter Eleven

Dom looked like a little boy who'd bought his mother what he believed was a diamond necklace from the school Christmas boutique, then found out it was paste. Sky wanted to put her arms around him.

"It's all my fault, Victoria." The words came tumbling out of her mouth as she slid forward, prepared to jump from the countertop.

Dom extended his arm. "No, you don't. Keep your weight off that ankle," he ordered.

"No way am I having this conversation sitting up here." She pushed at his arm but it was like trying to move a block of concrete.

Looking as angry as a wounded bear and as frustrated as a two-year-old told no, he encircled her waist with his hands and easily lifted her down.

"Will someone please explain to me what's going on?" Hands on hips, Victoria stood two feet away and looked directly at her.

Sky limped to the other side of the island and grabbed

the teakettle, filling it with water. Then she replaced it on the burner. "I'm going to make some tea. Want some?"

"I would love a cup," the other woman answered, following her and lifting cups from the cupboard. "Almost as much as I want to know what you two are up to. What is your fault?"

"Everything." Sky leaned her back against the counter and met the other woman's gaze. "Don't be angry at Dom."

"I don't need protection from a woman," he said. "I can take care of myself. I'm a big boy."

No argument there. He was definitely a man, she thought, remembering his wide wrists as he'd lifted her down. Every nerve ending in her body had been electrified when his muscles had bunched against the fabric of his white dress shirt as he'd easily taken her weight and set her on the floor. But he'd also administered first aid, blowing on the burning to ease her discomfort. How sweet was that? She studied his face, noting the dark growth of beard that shadowed his cheeks and jaw, adding "fierce" to his angry and frustrated expression.

There was also uneasiness in his eyes. Sky had seen it once before, when he'd spoken to the fireman's wife and son as he'd searched for the words to explain and minimize concern at the same time. He wore the look now as he regarded his mother, and Sky knew he was struggling for a way to not hurt her.

Finally he let out a long breath. "Sky is not to blame for any of this."

Her heart was full as she studied him, an amazing contradiction of power and tenderness. Then there was his integrity. No doubt about it. Hands down, he was the most remarkable man she'd ever known.

Victoria stared at her son, looking more confused than angry or upset. "I have so many questions I don't know where to start. That's not true. I do know. Your hand—Are you all right?"

"I'm fine." He flexed his fingers to show her. "But it's late, Mama. You need your rest. Your trip tomorrow—"

"I'm not going. How can I leave?"

Sky's heart caught. He might have pulled off the plan if Kenny hadn't shown up tonight. It was her fault his mother's trip was ruined. No doubt fate was having a good laugh at her expense.

She loved him, but when explanations were over, there wasn't a snowball's chance in hell she and Dom could ever have more than memories. All she could do was make sure his relationship with Victoria was okay.

"But why?" he asked. "There's no reason you can't go—"

"Don't, Dominic. You've never lied to me. Something is going on." She glanced at Sky then looked at her son. "You went after Sky when she left the party crying. I was concerned so I followed. I couldn't see much standing behind you the way I was. But I heard that man call her Sky Colton."

"Is that all, Mama? I can explain—"

"Can you? Your *abuelita* told me something funny was going on the day we arrived. But I thought she was being foolish because she doesn't like Shelby."

"She doesn't?" Dom asked, obviously surprised.

Victoria shook her head. "There was no reason to burden you with her opinion because I knew once she met your fiancée face-to-face she would change her mind. Then we met and Shelby—Sky—whoever you are—didn't seem to remember what she'd said in the e-mails. Mama was suspicious. But after that day in the emergency room, she never mentioned it again. She said Sky was perfect for you.''

''Is that so?'' His gaze shifted to Sky.

Her pulse kicked up and she felt a definite thumping in all the appropriate places. What did he want her to say? Nothing, she hoped. Because her mouth was too dry to form words.

''Quite so,'' Victoria said. ''Tonight, before you sent me to call the police, I heard what that man said. You told me your fiancée uses assumed names so she won't be recognized. Then tonight— All the commotion— That despicable man obviously recognized her and called her Sky Colton. Are Sky and Shelby Parker one and the same? Why did the police arrest that man? Is he after her? Dominic, are you in some kind of danger? How can I leave on a trip?'' she asked, throwing her hands in the air.

For a split second Sky had thought maybe there was hope of salvaging the situation. Pretend Sky Colton was a persona made up to throw off tabloid reporters. But she couldn't do it. That would only open up another can of worms. Something else for his mother to be concerned about. Sky couldn't let Victoria believe her only son was at risk in any way. Not for a lousy cruise.

The teakettle whistled as steam escaped. Wasn't that interesting timing? She was about to blow the lid off this charade. The interruption gave her a chance to gather her thoughts. After pouring the water over teabags in the cups, Sky limped across the kitchen and placed them on the table.

''I think we should sit,'' she said, and did so.

''It's about time you followed doctor's orders,'' Dom said. He took his mother's arm urging her to the table, then settled her across from Sky. He sat at the head, between them.

"Here's the deal." Sky took a deep breath, drawing strength from the reassuring look he gave her. "My name is Sky Colton. Really and truly. I'm a jewelry designer from Black Arrow, Oklahoma. Dom's fiancée, Shelby Parker, heard about me using Native American elements in my work and came to see me, to sketch original designs for her wedding bands. After several trips, she approved one. Then she came to Black Arrow and picked them up. But she seemed different, doubtful. I was busy, only half listening to what she was telling me. In response, I said something about everyone should follow their heart. That life is too short to waste more than a minute on anything that doesn't feel right."

The advice was sound, no matter that she'd been distracted when she'd said it. If Shelby had discovered she didn't love Dom, how could she go through with the ceremony? Any more than Sky could marry a man who didn't respect her heritage.

Sky lifted her teabag from the steaming liquid. "Apparently, Shelby didn't feel right about the marriage."

"Why did she not feel right?" Victoria directed the question to her. Before there was time to answer, she shot a look at her son. "Why did she not have an engagement ring?"

Sky put her hand up. She felt like the lion tamer trying to call attention away from targeted prey. "I'm sure the fact that Dom didn't have time to get an engagement ring had nothing to do with Shelby's feelings." She blew on her tea. "I know he loved Shelby. After spending time with him and seeing how important his work is, I have a better understanding of the depth of his emotions."

"As do I," the older woman said, looking at her son skeptically. "But there is still something that puzzles me. Why would she pretend to be Shelby?"

Dom ran a hand through his hair. "It was the only thing I could think of. You wouldn't go on the trip if you learned that my engagement was off. And I wanted you to go. After all you've done for me—"

"You are my son," she said simply. "But a ruse like this... It's not like you."

"It was my idea," Sky said. She felt his gaze on her and heat traveled up her neck and into her cheeks. But she rushed on before his integrity kicked in and he interrupted her. "Dom came to see me to settle the bill for the rings and he told me what happened. I felt badly about everything. It occurred to me that all he had to do was get through the engagement party, then you could take your cruise and have a wonderful time. Afterward, he could break the news."

"She's a liar, Mama."

"I am," Sky agreed, shooting him a glare. "Who better to pull this off? It took some fast talking, but I finally made him see it was as simple as doing the wrong thing for the right reason."

"She's a bad liar. Sky didn't want to be party to the deception, but I convinced her."

"You were very convincing," Victoria said, alternately studying Sky and her son. "Whoever talked who into what, I was fooled. Like two lovebirds, you were."

Sky knew now why that had been so easy. She loved him. Somehow it felt as though she always had. No way could she let him take the fall. She'd cost Dom the woman he loved and it was her fault their cover had been blown. She couldn't stand it if his relationship with his mother suffered because of her.

"If I had kept my opinions to myself, Dom would still be engaged to Shelby. She was perfect for him. I know you highly approved of the match."

"Shelby seemed perfect," the other woman agreed.

Until that moment Sky hadn't realized how much she'd hoped Dom's mother would dispute her statement. Her heart twisted and she caught her breath at the pain. With an effort, she pulled herself together. This wasn't about her feelings.

"Victoria, you have to take your trip. It means so much to Dom," she said, meeting his intense gaze. What was he thinking? Scratch that. She was probably better off not knowing. "You're a very lucky woman."

"Why do you say that?" she asked.

"You have one son, a respected doctor who took extraordinary measures to do something nice for you. I have five brothers and can't imagine any of them going to such great lengths to get my mother to take a trip. Maybe because most of them are in law enforcement. For the Coltons, it's practically a given."

"Except for you," Victoria pointed out.

"Yeah." She met the other woman's gaze. "Every family needs a black sheep. It's a dirty job, but someone had to do it."

"And you tried to help Dom pull the wool over my eyes."

"Good one," Sky said, a corner of her mouth curving up.

She couldn't manage a from-the-heart smile. Any slim chance she might have had to make Dom care about her even a little had died a slow and painful death tonight. What had made her think she could convince anyone she was an heiress? Why had she, even for a moment, thought she could pull this off? His mother had sacrificed everything for her son. She had a crystal-clear vision of who she wanted Dom to marry. And Calamity Colton wasn't even second runner-up. What a time to realize the woman wouldn't easily be fooled by an imposter. Not even an imposter who loved him.

Sky stood and picked up her cup, limping to the sink with it. Then she headed for the doorway, stopping by the table. "I'm pretty tired all of a sudden. And you two must have a million things to talk about."

"No." Victoria stood, also. "We'll talk in the morning, after I have had a chance to think." She kissed Dom's cheek. "Good night, my son. Sky," she said.

"Good night, Victoria."

Before she could follow the older woman from the room, Sky felt her arm caught in a steel grip. She met Dom's gaze. "Please let me go."

"I need to talk to you."

She shook her head. "There's nothing left to say."

"You're wrong."

"Yeah. I was wrong to think I could pull this off." She sighed. "It's time for me to leave, Dom. Tonight. Now that everything is out in the open, there's no reason to stay. I'll call Bram to pick me up. I'm going home with him."

"Sky—"

She pulled her arm from his grasp. "I'm sorry about everything. More than you'll ever know."

She walked out of the kitchen, hoping he would follow. Any promise she'd held for their future died when he didn't.

The next morning Dom flipped the switch on the coffeemaker, then turned his back and leaned against the counter. Almost instantly it started to sizzle and spit. Not unlike the way he was feeling. His eyes were raw and grainy. That happened when you didn't sleep all night. And then his mother and grandmother walked into the room.

"Where is Sky?" Isabel asked, sitting at the table. "It's not like her to let you make coffee."

Dom folded his arms across his chest, where a gnawing pain started. "She's gone."

"Gone? Where?" His mother stared at him from the doorway. "Don't we need to leave soon? For the ship?"

"You're going?"

"Of course," his grandmother said. "Victoria is now convinced that you can take care of your life."

He laughed and the sound was bitter. Once upon a time he'd been able to handle things. Not now. Not since Sky.

"Where did she go?" Victoria asked again. "She'll be back soon?"

He shook his head. "Sky went home to Black Arrow. With her cousin, Bram. He's the town sheriff. I met him at the police station last night, after he arrived to escort his prisoner back to Oklahoma."

"Why did she leave?" His grandmother glared at him. "What did you do, Dominic?"

"Didn't Mama tell you? The cat is out of the bag. The jig is up. The conspiracy is discovered." He ran a hand through his hair and gave in to his anger and frustration, hoping it would anesthetize the threatening pain. "She went back to her real life. She's not my fiancée."

"I knew that."

He frowned. "You knew? When? How?"

"Almost from the first." His grandmother smiled. "I didn't know what was going on, mind you. But that girl was not the young woman I wrote to. The one who would dispose of fine antiques and replace them with chrome, glass and black lacquer."

"Why didn't you say something?" he asked.

"I'm an old woman. I don't get out much. Life can be boring. It seemed far more entertaining to— How do you say it?" she asked, frowning. Then she smiled. "String you along."

Dom struggled to hold back a grin in spite of the depression that had snapped at him ever since Sky had left. "And?"

"And I was right. It was most entertaining watching the two of you. Cuddling, kissing. Snuggling. Being in love."

"We were only *pretending* to be in love."

"Maybe at first, although I have my doubts about that, too. More like love at first sight. Like your mama and papa. So you may have thought you were pretending, but I'm sure that very soon there was no pretending going on."

"Mama, what is she saying?" he asked.

She smiled. "I should think it's quite clear. Your grandmother means that we know you're in love with Sky Colton."

"That's not all," his grandmother interjected. "She loves you, too."

"And you discovered this—how?" He looked at each of them in turn.

"It started when I knew Shelby Parker was not the woman for you," the older woman said.

"Your grandmother is right." His mother shook her head. "I fear I'm to blame for you choosing unwisely. You heard me all these years saying how much I want you to have a better life. To marry a woman like the ones I worked for. You were trying to please me and you would have been most unhappy. I'm so very sorry, Dominic."

"You didn't force me to propose to Shelby."

"No. But because of me all you could see was her wealthy background and her busy life, which would keep her out of your hair."

Good wife material. That's exactly what he'd thought. He rubbed the back of his neck. "Shelby and I would have made a good match."

"What about Sky?" his mother asked.

"She's stubborn, opinionated. I firmly believe it's her goal in life to drive a man crazy, make him furious, and excited and—"

"Smile? Feel alive? Stimulated? Love?" his mother asked. "In short, isn't she the perfect wife for you?"

"How can you ask me that? I rushed into things with Shelby and you see how that went. I haven't known Sky but a few weeks—"

Victoria wagged her finger at him. "The length of time is not important. As your *abuelita* said, love at first sight, it runs in the family. I knew the first time I met your father that he was the love of my life. My heart was convinced there would never be another man for me. And there hasn't been. Did you ever wonder why I never remarried?"

"I just thought—"

"No one was interested?"

"Well, yes," he admitted.

She laughed. "I had opportunities. Men wanted me—"

"I don't want to hear this, Mama," he said, holding up his hand.

"There is nothing to hear. I couldn't think about any

other man. Your father was my heart's desire. Marrying for any other reason is wrong. When Sky said you couldn't find time for Shelby, I knew it wasn't love."

Dom thought back, to just before Shelby had eloped. She left messages for him that they needed to talk. For one reason or another, he'd stood her up. Work, office hours, emergencies. Everything else had come before her. Thank God she'd had the good sense not to marry him. He made a mental note to send her a wedding present. She'd done him a huge favor.

"Sky is the right woman for you." His mother nodded emphatically.

"How can you be so sure?"

Stupid question. The aching emptiness that opened up inside him the second she'd left was a big clue.

"You protected her at the risk of everything you and I worked all our lives for."

He knew what she meant. When he'd seen Sky at the mercy of that felon, he hadn't thought of anything but getting her away from him. "You mean, because I hit that son of a bitch who was going to hurt her?"

She nodded. "You could have damaged your hand. You might never have done surgery again."

"You're as dramatic as Sky."

"No." Victoria closed her eyes for a moment as she shook her head. "It was a risk and you didn't think about the consequences. You only knew that she was in danger and you had to do something."

"Yes," he agreed.

It was so simple, why hadn't he seen it for himself? He would do anything, give up anything, be anything for Sky Colton. Because he was in love with her.

"You must go after her," his grandmother insisted. "Convince her that she loves you, too."

He shook his head. "I don't know that I can persuade her of anything."

"Nonsense," the older woman scoffed. "She helped you with a ridiculous intrigue to get your mother on this trip. If she didn't love you, a forthright, honest young woman like her would have told you to take your plan and stick it in your ear."

"You have a way with words, *Abuelita.*" He chuckled.

"Don't laugh at your grandmother, Dominic. She's right. You must go after Sky. Soul mates don't grow on trees, you know."

He remembered Sky saying the same thing—about brides. But he would never forget the completely flat expression in her eyes just before she'd walked out the door. One of the things he loved most was her lively spirit, her contagious warmth. The way she would debate him about anything she truly believed. He feared she believed she wasn't the right woman for him.

"When are you leaving to see Sky?" his grandmother demanded.

He walked over to her and bent, kissing her cheek. "First I'm going to see you and Mama off on your cruise. Then I'm going to figure out what to do about Sky."

But he already knew. Somehow he would convince her that she was not just right, she was absolutely the *only* woman for him.

Chapter Twelve

With a sketchpad in front of her, Sky sat behind the counter in her shop. She often diddled with design ideas while minding the store, especially when things were slow. As they were now.

Slow sort of described her personal life, as well. Although it was a welcome relief, particularly after her close call with Kenny in Houston. Thinking of the city where Dom lived brought a fresh wave of pain and sadness. *That* was not a welcome relief. But it had only been two days since she'd seen him. Time healed all wounds. Though she had a bad feeling a whole lifetime wouldn't be enough time to get over him.

The first night he'd brought her to his home, she'd hoped by the time she returned to Black Arrow his pain and the loneliness he'd felt after losing his fiancée would be less. Little had she known that she would be taking the feelings home with her. That happened when you knew you'd never have the only man you'd ever love.

Her full of promise? Grandpa George's mystical wires must have been crossed.

Sighing, she looked at her pad, with the initials D.R. written on it. "Dominic Rodriguez," she whispered. Then she wrote Mrs. D.R. "Mrs. Dr. Dominic Rodriguez."

Not in this lifetime, she thought. A shudder started in her chest and worked its way up, lodging as a sob in her throat. Just then the door opened and in walked Bram with her brother Grey.

The two men were similar in height, with Grey about an inch above their cousin's six feet. Both had black hair and eyes, but the likeness stopped there. Bram was dressed in his tan sheriff's uniform and exuded a more laid back Western demeanor. Her brother was the complete opposite—from his short-styled hair, navy suit, red tie and long-sleeved white shirt all the way to his black-tasseled loafers. Grey Colton was every inch the conservative judge.

"Hello," she said, then cleared her throat to dislodge the emotion. Quickly she flipped her sketchpad closed.

"Hey, Sky." Bram walked over and rested his hands on the counter.

Grey followed, standing in front of her. "Hi, sis."

"What are you guys doing here?" Then she had a horrible thought. "Are things okay with Mom and Dad?" she asked Grey.

He shrugged. "The usual. She has one nerve left and since his retirement, he's getting on it."

Sky shook her head and sighed. "I sure hope they'll be okay."

"Me, too. But that's not why we're here."

She met her brother's gaze. "Please say you didn't come here to tell me Kenny escaped."

"No." Bram looked at the other man. "He's going to stand trial. Justice will be done."

Grey nodded. "It will be swift and sure if I'm the one who hears his case."

The other man grinned. "Although good old-fashioned frontier justice wouldn't be a bad thing for a weasel like him, I think if his case lands in your court, it might be a conflict of interest."

"Yeah. It pains me to admit it, but I'd have to recuse myself."

Sky studied them. "Did you guys have another reason for coming here? Or did you just need neutral territory for this conversation?"

Grey rubbed the back of his neck. "There is some bad news."

She instantly thought of Dom and her chest tightened. It didn't matter that she was nothing to him. If anything happened to him it would tear her apart. Worse, if anything happened to him, no one would notify her. Their relationship, such as it was, was on a need-to-know basis. She had no right to know anything about what was up with him. But that didn't change the fact that she would always need to know he was okay.

"What's wrong?" she asked.

"I got a call from California," Bram started. "Joe Colton Junior has been in an accident."

"Oh, no," she said, touching her fingers to her mouth. "This family has been through so much, both the California Coltons and us here in Oklahoma. Now that Kenny's in jail, I thought all the bad stuff was behind us." She looked from one man to the other. "What happened?"

Grey sighed. "The information is sketchy. Joe is in

the hospital and they're doing tests. That's all I know right now."

"You'll tell me when you have news?" she asked.

Her brother nodded. "I'll make sure you get the memo."

"Good." Sky looked at both of them. "Is there anything else? Maybe a meteor heading toward earth? The ice cap is melting? A natural disaster the likes of which mankind has never seen?"

Grey studied her, one eyebrow rising. "Testy today, aren't we?"

"This doom and gloom wouldn't happen to have anything to do with a certain Houston doctor, would it, Miss Crabby Pants?" Bram asked.

She laughed, or at least tried to. The sound was more groan than giggle because her heart was breaking. She missed Dom terribly. Trying to hide her feelings was a tall order because her cousin, the sheriff, was too perceptive by far. Finally she opted to act like a child.

"I'm not crabby," she snapped.

"O-o-kay." The two men exchanged skeptical glances, then turned their gazes on her.

"Did you come here to pick on me? If so, I'm a busy woman. I've got things to do, people to see, jewelry to design."

Before she knew what was happening, her brother grabbed her pad and flipped it open. "D.R.? Doctor? Mrs. D.R.? Do the initials stand for someone in particular?" He looked at Bram. "You're the sheriff. What do you make of this?"

"Give that back," she demanded, making a grab. But Grey easily moved it out of her reach. "I'll tell Mom on you."

"She's bringing in the big guns. I think I hit a nerve,"

Grey observed. ''What's up, sis? Does Bram need to beat someone up for you? I'd do it myself, but how would it look if a judge was the muscle for his sister?''

Bram leaned his elbows on the glass jewelry case and studied her. ''Does this someone have the initials Dominic Rodriguez?'' He glanced at Grey. ''Now that I think about it, in Houston she was like a mother lion defending her cub when I came down on the doc.''

''Oh, for Pete's sake,'' she complained. ''Don't you guys have anything better to do than harass me? Bad guys to catch, perps to send up the river?''

''Actually,'' Bram said, ''I'm here to buy something for Jenna.''

''Is it her birthday?'' Sky asked, relieved to have the focus off her and her dismal love life.

He shook his head. ''Nope. And before you ask, I didn't do anything to upset her. She's just hormonal. What with the pregnancy and all.''

''That's so sweet,'' she said, her eyes prickling as tears threatened to gather. Apparently his wife wasn't the only one with raging hormones. ''Do you see anything you like?'' she asked, indicating her display case.

He pointed. ''These silver and turquoise earrings—the ones that look like raindrops.''

From her side she slid open the glass door to the case and reached inside to pull them out. ''You have excellent taste. They would look lovely with Jenna's Anglo coloring.''

Bram examined them, then met her gaze. ''That's an interesting way to say she has blond hair and blue eyes. I sense something going on with you. *Is* it about the doctor? Anything to do with the fact that you're part Comanche?''

''No.'' She shook her head, but understood Bram's

sensitivity on the subject. Jenna's father had been opposed to their relationship because of his Indian blood. "This is about the fact that I wouldn't fit in his world."

"Don't sell yourself short, sis," Grey advised. "Just because that guy you almost married is a jerk, doesn't mean someone out there won't think the sun rises and sets on you."

"Right. And any minute now I'll flap my arms and fly."

"I'll take these." Bram handed her the earrings. "Your brother is right about that sun rising and setting thing. But in case that's not enough for you, I'm going to pass along what George WhiteBear said to me."

"Oh, please. Not more nonsense about me being full of promise."

"Don't scoff," he warned. "He's a wise old man."

"I'll give you the old part," she said as they stared at each other for several moments. She gave in first. "Okay. What did he say?"

"He advised me not to hide behind my heritage to save my heart. And he was right. I tried to resist Jenna because I was afraid of being hurt."

"You? Afraid?" She laughed, snapping the lid on the black velvet box.

"It's true. I'd take on a perp any day of the week and twice on Sunday. But falling for Jenna scared the life out of me."

Sky put the box in a gift bag and handed it to him. "I'll bill you."

One corner of his mouth turned up. "Shouldn't the advice I just gave you be an even trade?"

"It would be if you'd thought of it on your own." No way would she confirm how close to the truth he'd come. She'd tried to resist Dom. But even the fear of another rejection because of her heritage hadn't stopped her from falling for him. That thought brought a fresh wave of pain. She wished they would leave so she could be alone. "Jenna will love the earrings. She's a lucky woman."

"I think so." He put the small package in his shirt pocket and headed for the door.

Grey leaned on the counter and grinned at their cousin. "Colton conceit."

"Don't look now, Grey," she said. "But your envy is showing."

"No way, little sister. What you see is relief. Single and satisfied."

She shook her head at her big brother. "Always the lone wolf, as Grandpa likes to call you. Haven't you ever heard the expression 'pride goes before a fall'?"

"If I was you, I'd resuscitate my own love life before dispensing advice." Grey followed Bram to the door.

"There's nothing to resuscitate," she said honestly.

He glanced outside and looked down the street, then back at her. "Never say never." Then he walked out.

"'Bye, Sky. Thanks," Bram said, following her brother.

Sky looked around the empty shop for several moments trying to decide whether or not she was better off crabby with company or alone and sad. She decided keeping busy was the best therapy and grabbed the glass cleaner. After slipping out from behind the counter, she squirted some of the liquid on the front of the case, then started wiping it off with a paper towel. There were sticky fingerprints, kids' lip marks and smears she didn't want to identify.

Behind her, the door opened. Probably family members come to torment her again.

"I'm warning you. If you're here to pick on me—"

"You don't look like a home wrecker."

Sky froze. At least on the outside. Inside her pulse skittered because her heart boogied big-time at the sound of the familiar deep voice. She straightened slowly and turned, letting her eyes confirm what her ears and heart already knew.

Dominic Rodriguez.

There he stood in jeans, boots and black leather jacket, looking tall, dark, and dangerous. His blue eyes oozed intensity. For the life of her she couldn't figure out why he was still on that home-wrecker kick. It was obvious he and Shelby hadn't loved each other. She'd done him a favor by running off with the chauffeur.

Her hands shook along with her legs. "I don't look like a home wrecker because I'm not."

"Yes, you are."

"If this is about Shelby, I need to say once and for all that you're better off without her. There are so many clues I can't even tell you. You've got to let it go."

"I already have. But there's someone I can't let go."

"W-who?" she asked, heart pounding.

"You. If you leave me, you will be a home wrecker."

She blinked up at him. "I don't believe you."

"It's true, Sky. After you left I realized a lot of things. One of which was that Shelby tried to break it off. She kept making dates with me to talk, but I stood her up every time. Work always came before her. Sometimes it needed to, emergencies are part of the job. But sometimes it didn't, and that's not good enough. She was right to end it."

"Okay, then." She stared, drinking in everything about him—his wonderful thick, black hair, his tall, strong body, the scent of his skin. A sensory stockpile for the rest of her life. "I don't understand why you came all this way to tell me that—" Her eyes widened as she realized what day it was. "What about office hours?"

"Canceled."

"But your appointments—"

"Rescheduled."

"On call?"

"A colleague is covering for me."

"Why?"

"Because nothing is more important than seeing you."

"I don't get it. Your mother and grandmother must hate me."

"They told me I was a fool if I didn't go after you."

"Really?" When he nodded she said, "But I'm all wrong for you."

He ran a hand through his hair and the intensity in his eyes cranked up. "Look, Sky, I'm not the jerk who hurt you. Don't punish me for what he did. Don't hide behind that to keep me at arm's length."

She thought about what Bram had said, the words of wisdom from George WhiteBear. Was she hiding behind her heritage? Pushing Dom away because she was afraid?

She set the spray bottle on the countertop and stuck her hands in her pockets. "But we haven't known each other very long. Look what happened with you and Shelby."

"According to my mother the length of time you know someone is not a prerequisite for love—if you meet the right someone. Why did you run out of our engagement party?"

"First of all, it wasn't ours and that was beginning to

get to me. Then your grandmother asked me when I knew I'd fallen in love with you."

"You didn't answer her."

"Because I—"

"Don't love me?"

"No. I mean, yes. I mean—"

"I'll tell you when *I* knew," he said, moving closer. "When I saw that bastard threatening to hurt you. The thought of losing you forever scared the hell out of me. That's when I knew I loved you."

"It did? You do?" She wanted so badly to believe.

"Yes. Now it's your turn. Why did you run?"

"I hated myself for deceiving them. I couldn't stand it anymore. They're so sweet and funny. I started caring about them and I hated the lying."

"It wasn't exactly a lie. My grandmother knew almost from the first that we were pulling a fast one. And I realized something when my mother made the comment about this elaborate ruse being out of character for me."

"So you're not a liar. So what?"

"It's not like me at all. But I had to do it. That was all I could think of to keep you in my life. I couldn't walk away and never see you again. I guilted you into going along with the plan so I could bring you to Houston."

"And what about not telling me your mother knew Shelby had moved in?"

"Not exactly deliberate. Certainly not my finest hour. And believe it or not, it was out of character. I figured I was losing my mind. That was easier to believe than the truth— I was falling in love with you."

"But you thought you loved Shelby, too. Why should I believe you feel differently about me?"

"For one thing, you didn't elope with your chauffeur."

"If I had one, and he was you..."

She tried very hard not to smile, but failed miserably. In fact her attempt to resist him was doomed to failure. With every fiber of her being, she was certain she loved this man. If she'd known him four minutes, four hours, four days, four months, or forty years, she would still love him forever.

"I came home to Black Arrow because I have a business to run."

"Can you run it from Houston?"

"Yes. I was thinking about branching out to a larger city. But why? What are you saying?"

He rested his hands on the glass counter, one on either side of her, trapping her. "I want to spend the rest of my life with you. You make me laugh. I like coming home to you. No one has ever made me as angry as you. I enjoy arguing with you, talking with you, kissing you. There is a perfect woman for me and she's you. This is different from how I felt about Shelby because when she left I was almost relieved. When you walked out the other night, I felt—desolate, alone, lost. It was as if the sun, moon and stars had been removed from my Sky."

"Oh, Dom—"

He took her face in his palms and stared into her eyes for several moments, as if he couldn't believe she was there. Then he lowered his mouth to hers and kissed her sweetly, but she felt his hands trembling.

When he pulled away, his breathing was ragged. "I love you, Sky Colton."

"I love you right back, Dominic Rodriguez."

"I promised you if you helped me with my plan I

would do something for you. But you couldn't think of anything you wanted."

"I remember," she said, meeting his gaze. She smiled. "But it was my fault our cover was blown. So maybe the deal is off?"

"Not a chance. My mother and grandmother left on the cruise the day before yesterday."

"Oh, Dom, I'm glad. They must have been so excited. I wish I could have seen them off."

He cleared his throat. "So you see, we achieved our objective. I owe you. It's time to call in your favor rain check. There must be something I can do for you."

"There is." She pressed her palm against his chest and felt his hammering heart. StoneHeart? No way. He was a flesh-and-blood man who was warm and caring and she took strength from him. "Marry me."

"That's not a favor. It's my greatest desire."

"Dr. Rodriguez, a simple yes or yes will suffice."

"Yes."

He reached into the pocket of his leather jacket and pulled out a ring. Taking her left hand, he slipped on the emerald she'd left with him in Houston.

He held her at arm's length as he met her gaze. "All my life I've worked to make my mother proud, have more than when I was a child, give her the things she wanted. I set goals. Tried to be the best. But it was never enough. And now I know why. I was always reaching for my Sky."

"Corny as that is, I love you, Dom, more than I knew it was possible to love anyone."

"You are the missing piece of my heart. You make me whole. You fill my life with love and promise."

"That's me—Sky full of promise."

In spite of her teasing words, tears gathered in her

eyes. He pulled her against him and she knew it was where she belonged. Her black sheep days were behind her. She would never feel out of place.

In Dom's arms, the fit was perfect.

* * * * *